Psychic Princess

#1: Admirable Avocation

By

Jolinda Pizzirani

www.SummerlandPublishing.com

SUMMERLAND
PUBLISHING

First Edition July, 2004

ISBN: 978-0-9794585-2-1

Printed in the U. S. A.

Chapter One

The rain was falling steadily outside her bedroom window. Danni pulled back the shutters to watch the colorful patterns forming as the drops fell amongst her carefully planted flowerbeds. The trees and foliage around her house were green with springtime growth and she smiled as she thought of how desperately this rain was needed. Santa Bella was her hometown; she had grown up here before moving to LA during her college days, and had always held a special love for this unique, beautiful place. Nestled between the beautiful Pacific Ocean and the majestic mountains, Santa Bella was carefully shielded from big industry and sprawling growth.

She had purchased her secluded ranch-style home seven years ago because of it's proximity to the ocean -- she could easily hike the short distance to the beach where she spent many peaceful hours. And, because huge trees and foliage surrounded the house, she felt secure and secluded from the eyes, *and minds,* of others. *Until recently.*

Danni put aside her rambling thoughts and concerns, and turned to face her guest who sat across the room, patiently waiting for her to continue speaking.

"You see, I'm psychic." There. She had said it out loud. She was somewhat surprised when this statement didn't elicit any kind of response at all from her guest, Dr. Richard Smith, a respected psychiatrist she had grudgingly turned to for help in sorting out her complicated life. She studied the doctor for a moment: a mature man in his late fifties, tanned, fit and totally gray, but quite attractive in a professional sort of way. Yet, she decided, a little *too* professional for her taste. She shrugged, and then went on to try and describe her unique capabilities.

"In my case, that means I seem to be able to pick up on other people's thoughts and well, *their vibrations* -- but only *some* of the time." That just about covers everything, she thought contritely. He'll probably sign the papers to send me to the loony bin any minute now. Maybe if she tried to explain it a little more. "See, it's far from being a 'perfect science' -- in fact, it's quite the opposite. I guess that's why I've sought seclusion to a certain degree--it helps to keep my mind 'uncluttered'."

Danni's smile faded when she noticed the doctor was busily making notes in his large, black notebook. Probably documenting his upcoming formal opinion of her certifiability, she thought ruefully. When he finished and looked at her expectantly, she continued, thoughtfully. "When I was in college and in full recognition of my...ah...talent, I nearly drove myself mad trying to sort out all of the sensations I was constantly receiving. I had lots of friends then...or I *thought* they were friends. Many were only interested in *using* me, I soon found out. People with lost personal items and questions about things like their love lives and their upcoming tests flooded my mind to the point where I almost dropped out when I couldn't find time for my own studies."

Her face grew wistful, and she tucked her feet under her, hugging a pillow as she let her memories flow freely forth. Her lips curled into a smile. "Then I met Sam. He was a graduate student in Political Science who found me wandering aimlessly around campus one day. He told me later I looked like a bewildered lost puppy, which was the reason he stopped to see if I was all right, then we sat and talked for hours. Finally, I had met a person who *understood* me, and he wasn't the least bit fazed by my psychic ability. In fact, he treated it as a natural extension of my personality and left it at that. It was so refreshing -- I loved it -- and him. I'm convinced that he saved my sanity, and I certainly give him credit for my graduating with honors two years later."

She laid the pillow aside, and sighed heavily, totally lost now in her thoughts. "By that time, though, we had both grown and matured, and realized quite simply that our lives were destined to part." She looked up and smiled, content with the outcome of her first special relationship. "We still write each other occasionally, and always at Christmas. He's married now, very happily, with three kids and a fourth on the way. I tease him that I always knew he was a 'fast worker,'" she smiled contentedly. "I'm just eternally glad I met him when I did, and shared the time we had together."

Danni became aware suddenly that she was getting off-track, but her guest merely nodded and said simply "Go on," in indication she should continue in the same vein. She figured this was the stuff you were supposed to talk about to a shrink, anyway, so what the heck. "After Sam, my love life was pretty tame...a few flings here and there, you know what I mean?" This prompted a smile and a nod, but nothing further.

"Anyway, you may not believe it, but it's a terrible burden to have this kind of *ability*, as I like to call it -- although I sometimes wonder if it isn't more of a *disability*. She giggled, then stopped when she saw the doctor's indulgent look. "I've known about my '*inner mind*' -- that's another favorite term of mine -- since I was about four or five. I used to have a wonderful time irritating my friends -- especially my brother -- by anticipating their every move. When it came to chess and checkers I was unbeatable. It wasn't funny, though, when everybody stopped playing with me and started calling me names. My mom tried to tell me it was just their way of expressing their jealousy of my "*uniqueness*", and that I shouldn't take it personally." Danni shook her head, and scrunched up her face at her unpleasant recollections.

"I would cry and call them a bunch of sore losers, and my mother would gather me close and say, 'Now, now, princess, I've told you before that God gives each of us something special to use to help others during our lives. Sometimes its difficult to learn what that something special is and just how best to use it, but we each must try our very best.'

"She would pat my head encouragingly, and drift off to get ready for whatever tea or party she was invited to that particular day. Oh, don't misunderstand, I love my mother dearly, but I learned very early in life that she was a bit *different* from all my friends' moms. For one thing, she had been married and divorced--or widowed--<u>five</u> times by the time I was eight years old. Which, by the way, is how I got the nickname of 'Princess'." Danni realized she was really on a roll now, but couldn't stop herself from spilling out her entire life history in one sitting, it seemed.

"You see, my full name is Danniella Luisa Celestina Speranza, from my mother's second husband -- my father -- an Italian diplomat who had the misfortune of dying from a heart attack when I was two. Anyway, it was either her third or fourth husband who had the questionable title of Duke or some such thing, and from then on she insisted I be considered of royal heritage too -- so I got the nickname of "Princess". To me it was all part of the fun of growing up in the glittering, exciting -- if occasionally confusing -- world of my beautiful, wild mother in her search for eternal happiness and bliss."

The Doctor wrote another short note, then said "Interesting," and again looked at Danni expectantly. Pulling herself back to the subject at hand, Danni became serious once again. "Back to my psychic tendencies -- my mom thought that I was simply an exceptionally bright child who had a natural ability to reason what the future held. She never, in her entire life, acknowledged the existence of any "psychic" capability or, for that matter, any other unknown phenomenon. So, I was forced at an early age to experiment on my own and come to my own conclusions about my strange abilities.

"One thing I found out right away was that I couldn't ever foresee my own future or anything to do with myself. When I was little, I could sit and concentrate until my head hurt, trying to determine what my grades would be, but it was no use. I could be about to be hit by a Mack truck and nonchalantly keep walking straight into it's path. Thank heavens I'm not a daydreamer as well, and seem to have quite ordinary senses when it comes to the normal five we all have." She chortled out loud, but her hopeful spurt of laughter died when the psychiatrist merely nodded his understanding.

"Anyhow, my life until recently had been fairly routine -- for a person like me, that is. After graduating from college with an Art Major, I worked in several non-potential, relatively boring jobs with companies in the LA area. Then about six years ago, my grandfather died and left my brother and I a sizable estate which we promptly divided equally and went our separate ways -- he to the slopes of Colorado, and me to my oceanside Santa Bella home. Mother, at that time, was somewhere off the coast of Spain, living with a dark and terribly handsome man whom she said 'dabbled' in hotels.

"I've spent the last six years happily living a life which I thought was perfect -- painting, sculpting, writing some light poetry, entertaining occasionally, and volunteering from time to time." She leaned forward and added meaningfully, "I also love gourmet cooking and jump at the chance to practice on others." She realized this might have sounded like an overt invitation, and hoped the good doctor was not of a mind to take her up on her suggestion. It was immediately apparent that he was not, and she felt like laughing at herself, then managed to go on with her story.

"Mine was a solitary existence, except for the company of my two dogs – Zara and Tequila, three cats – Sofia, Mecio and Nera, and my turtle, Max." She smiled as she rattled off the names of her pets with love and warmth. "But then my happy, peaceful life changed drastically -- beginning about six months ago today..."

Chapter Two

Danni carried in the last bag of groceries from her favorite market where she always seemed to buy tons of high-priced gourmet goodies, sure that she would be needing them for an unexpected guest who might appear at her door.

As she passed by her sunny art studio off the living room, she stopped for a moment to study her latest attempt at a sculpture, and shook her head in dismay. She was proud that her last seven sculptures had been commissioned by a well-known designer for placement in his client's homes and offices. Personally, she just enjoyed the creative process of using her hands and fingers to produce a work of art that someone else might like. Chastising herself for being less than productive lately, she mentally decided to get back to work on it as soon as she was finished with the groceries.

She was busy finding a proper place to store the fresh basil, pine nuts, garlic and imported parmesan cheese she would make into a delicious pesto sauce, when the phone rang. As usual, her mind clicked on automatic and she knew before picking it up that it was her dear friend, Peggy.

"Hi Peggy. How's your throat?" Danni heard a decisive snort of disgust on the other end of the line.

"Better, thanks. I'm still taking the antibiotics the doctor put me on." Peggy sneezed loudly, then complained, "You know I hate that, Danni. You could at least *pretend* that you don't know it's me, for goodness sake." Her voice turned into a pleading whine. "Just once -- to please me?"

Danni laughed at her friend's irritation good naturedly, realizing things hadn't really changed that much since she was a kid after all.

"Sorry, pal. I'll try to remember next time...really. It's just hard sometimes -- the words pop out before I can stop them."

"Well," Peggy said grudgingly, "it's bound to get you in trouble one day. You remember how upset that cute guy was at your last dinner party. I can't blame him for being mad when you asked about his being called 'string bean' as a child. How could you? Especially to a hunk like him."

"I know, I know. But I apologized later, and by his response, I'm *sure* he forgave me ... if you know what I mean."

Peggy sighed with exasperation. "You're incorrigible. I give up. I can't even find one lousy date, and you have men crawling all over you, even when you embarrass them in front of a whole group of people."

Danni laughed easily. "They're not exactly *crawling* on me, Peg. After all, you know I'm very picky when it comes to men. I just haven't met the right guy yet...they're all so shallow and self-absorbed. Besides, I'm saving myself for my knight in shining armor -- if I ever meet him, that is."

"Sure," Peggy answered sarcastically, "I know how you are. But take my advice: you'd better stop being so damn 'picky', as you call it, or you'll end up an old maid like me. And if you're smart, you'll keep your little *psychic insights* about them to yourself too -- you scare away every guy that's attracted to you that way."

As usual, Danni grew quickly tired of this type of conversation. After all, she was who she was. Either she would find someone who accepted her this way, or forget it. She couldn't change, she knew that for sure. She had tried, and failed.

"So what's really up, anyway? I'm sure you called for some reason other than to harass me about my private life. Are you calling from work?"

Peggy worked as a salesgirl in a trendy little shop in the middle of town. Danni had met her about two years before when shopping for a party dress for New Year's Eve. They had hit it off immediately and became fast friends, even though they had little in common. Peggy was short, a little on the heavy side, with bright red hair and tons of freckles. She tried to tame her wild curly hair with different styles and accessories, but she still always managed to look as if she had just walked through the eye of a hurricane. And her clothes were not much better. She loved all the latest styles, but her body was just not made for them, and she therefore looked even more "robust" than ever.

Poor Peggy envied Danni's 5'8" frame, which she maintained at a steady 120 pounds without noticeable effort. Then there was Danni's thick black shoulder-length hair and lavender eyes which even Danni admitted were her best assets -- besides her long shapely legs which drew admiring glances wherever she went. Danni never worried much about her appearance...it was just *there*, and she felt sorry for her friend who struggled so hard to look good. Poor, dear Peggy.

"Yeah...and I'm starving. It's not even ten o'clock and I could eat a horse. I started that new diet I told you about...you know, all fruit for three days, then fasting for two days? Well, I'm only into my third hour of fruit, and I'm sick of it. Wanna go to lunch? How about Christian's Continental Restaurant over on Montecito and Bath Streets for some gooey pasta and heavenly garlic bread?"

"Peggy. Come on, now. You have more willpower than that, don't you?"

"No. Now what time shall we meet? 12:00? 12:30? Or even sooner..."

Danni gave in easily to her crazy friend, knowing Peggy would pig out for lunch no matter if she went or not, and maybe she could temper Peggy's appetite to some extent if she forced a salad down her throat first. They agreed to meet at noon, and Danni hung up and went back to putting away the last of her grocery items, humming happily.

Her life was so plain and ordinary and she was more than happy with it that way. She had friends, a few dates now and then, her wonderful home, and her pets. Period. No problems, no troubles -- *until that day.*

Danni was just deciding which pair of shoes to wear with her jeans and sweater when she got goose bumps all over her arms, and a strong sensation deep inside that she had never experienced before. She had always felt so safe in her Faith Ranch home, even though it was far removed from the main roads. She just never thought she needed any type of alarm system or protection -- a decision she was soon to be very sorry for.

She quickly shoved her stocking feet into some casual shoes, and turned from the closet to walk through the bedroom and into the hallway. Even the hairs on the back of her neck were at attention now -- something was definitely wrong. Still not hearing a single noise in the quiet house -- the dogs were outside, and her cats were sound asleep on the sofa -- she tiptoed towards the kitchen, opening the swinging door carefully. Her eyes scanned the room, her favorite in the house next to her art studio, and she saw nothing out of order. But there was something eerily disconcerting. "Stop being foolish, Danni," she chided herself out loud. Then, reassuring herself that she was simply imagining things -- another thing she would never do in the future -- she picked up her purse and headed for the garage.

When Danni got to the restaurant, Peggy was already seated and happily buttering a huge chunk of fragrantly fresh, warm sourdough bread. She smiled impishly and nodded toward the seat across from her.

"I don't want to hear it, ok Danni? I just give up, that's all. I'll always be frumpy and you'll always be gorgeous and I've finally come to accept that. So let me eat my meal in peace." At that Peggy took a huge bite of the bread, her cheeks bulging, her lips smeared with butter.

Danni laughed and shook her head. "I wasn't going to say a thing. I've always told you if you'd stop worrying so much about your weight, you'd probably lose it gradually and naturally. So don't jump all over me." Danni pretended to be quite hurt by her friend's words.

Peggy put down the bread and wiped her mouth with her napkin, looking slightly sheepish. "I know. I'm sorry I snapped at you. It must be all that damn fruit I ate this morning."

They both giggled, then hugged, and finally grabbed the menus to select their favorite items from the extensive list. Danni ordered a bottle of crisp, dry white Italian wine to complement their meal, and they settled down to enjoy their chat. Little did Danni know that this "chat" was about to change her entire future.

"I really had another reason for inviting you for lunch today, you know -- besides an excuse for chucking my diet," Peggy began mysteriously.

"Really? What?" Danni's inner mind clicked into gear, and she again felt that same distinctly unpleasant feeling that she had experienced before leaving home.

The words began pouring out of Peggy's mouth, as if she was afraid to stop to take a breath. "Well, there are these friends of mine -- actually they're closer friends to my mom and dad -- but anyway they've had the most awful thing happen. Their fifteen-year-old daughter has disappeared. And the police haven't been able to find out a thing -- they're treating it as a runaway -- not a kidnapping. I just can't believe it. I mean, I didn't know the girl that well personally, but I met her several times and she didn't seem the type to run away like that, or even the kind of kid to get that upset about anything. And her dad is just devastated -- her mom too, of course -- and I was telling them about you and your *thing* that you do, you know, and how *good* you are at it, and that maybe you could..."

Danni saw immediately where her friend was headed, and put her palm up to stop her mid-sentence. "Wait a minute, Peg, I admit I may have a *thing,* as you call it, but I certainly never suggested that I was any type of *professional* or anything. Why, just this morning on the phone you were telling me to keep my mouth shut about my psychic abilities." She couldn't believe her friend sometimes. "Good grief. Are you crazy? Those poor parents are in enough pain without bringing in strangers to muddle things up. I'm sure the police are doing everything they possibly can."

Peggy's face grew red and her eyes narrowed accusingly. "Look, Danni, I know what I said this morning. That was only about the men in your life, and I still say you should clam up in that department. I realize that I've always told you I hated it when you *knew* things about me and everyone else, but now I really believe this is an opportunity for you to do some *good* -- you could help these people find their daughter -- I *KNOW* you could. Remember when you found Mrs. Casey's missing dog? And what about all those times you knew right where I had left my car keys or my purse?"

"Please, Peggy. Don't compare dogs and keys and purses with a *missing child*. This is way out of my league. I just don't know..." Danni began, uncertainty heavy in her voice. Yet the thought of a young girl out there somewhere, maybe in terrible danger... The dull uncomfortable feeling was now growing into a huge lump of pain in her chest. She began to wonder if it was being caused by this whole conversation.

"Well, I do, and I think you should at least go to see these people...they're desperate for any help they can get -- honestly. Please?" Peggy leaned forward, pleadingly. *"For me?"*

Against her better judgment, Danni reluctantly agreed. "Okay, but only a short visit. I probably won't sense anything and it will all be a waste of their time and mine. But I suppose if there's even a small chance I could be of help, I should at least try..." Strangely, Danni realized the tightness in her chest was abruptly lessening.

"That's great. Oh, I'm so proud of you Danni. My best friend is going to save the day, I just know it." Peggy looked positively ecstatic, then seeing the uncertainty creep back into Danni's eyes at her exuberance, she added demurely, "I mean, I'm sure you'll do your *best* to help, that's all anyone could ask."

They were served their lunches, and after Peggy reluctantly agreed to forego the "Chocolate Decadence" dessert, the rest of the conversation was inconsequential. They agreed to meet the following morning and go to visit the home of the missing young girl. Danni now noticed that not only was the pain in her chest totally gone, but she actually began to feel a new sense of purpose -- another feeling she would certainly recognize and try to temper in the future.

Chapter Three

The sun was back shining brightly when Peggy picked Danni up at eight o'clock sharp the next morning in her little yellow sports car, and they zoomed along with the top down and the music blaring -- Peggy's standard procedure when driving. They followed Cabrillini Boulevard past the center of town, then drove for some distance further up into the hills of Montecello. Danni was beginning to wonder if Peggy knew where she was going, when she pulled into a long, winding driveway off Sheffy Drive flanked by massive gates mounted in an impressive, ten-foot tall stone enclosure around the property.

The grounds were beautifully maintained, and Danni admired the artistry of the placement of the lush green trees and flowering shrubs. She thought to herself that they must surely have a full-time gardener to keep things looking this nice, and at the same instant noticed a man kneeling in a flower patch, tenderly working with some new plants. He looked up as they passed, and Danni instantly felt a sharp impression of sadness as she looked into his eyes. The feeling passed as quickly as it came.

As they drew closer to the huge home, Danni panicked, and almost screamed aloud "What am I *doing here?*" Sure, she had had some luck occasionally helping people find missing items, but maybe it was just all a fluke. How many times had she had this same doubt. Yet, when she would continue to hear and see things with her mind -- things that would later come true in many instances -- she had to believe in herself once again or, and this was a distinct possibility, believe that she was totally and completely nuts.

Her mind was pulled back to the present as they pulled up to a stop, and Danni switched her attention to the beautiful home before them. If she had not known better, she would have sworn this was the house used to film *Gone With The Wind* -- Tara itself, only larger. The impressive white columns in front were mounted on a large entry staircase leading up to the massive front doors. The white paint on the exterior looked as fresh as if it had been applied only yesterday, with pots and planters of colorful flowers placed everywhere.

"Some place, huh?" Peggy said, noting the impression in Danni's eyes.

"I'll say. Who are these people anyway, the Rockefellers?"

Peggy laughed, and reached out to ring the doorbell, which chimed the beginning bars of a famous sonata. "Nah, just the Piedmonts. Nancy and Bill. Their daughter's name is Jessica. One kid, that's it. Bill's a lawyer, Nancy's a ...well, I guess you could call her a 'socialite', for lack of a better word."

Danni nodded and began to respond, but shut her mouth abruptly when the door opened and a kind-faced woman of Mexican descent smiled down at them. "Senorita Peggy, come in. And you have brought an amiga?"

Peggy pushed Danni in ahead of her, and turned to answer the woman. "Yes, Maria, this is my best friend, Danni."

"Danny?" Maria seemed confused at what she thought was a man's name.

"Short for Danniella," Danni offered quickly, and saw the comprehension in the woman's face.

"Oh, sí, I understand. But for me, I will call you Senorita Danniella, if you please, okay?"

"Sure, that's fine," Danni assured her. She realized suddenly that she sensed the same feeling of sadness surrounding Maria as she had felt emanating from the gardener outside. It was almost like Maria had *personally* been the one to suffer the loss of a daughter -- not her employers. She thought again of the gardener, then she realized that they had both probably been very close to Jessica and that would naturally explain their apparent unhappiness.

At that moment, a stylishly elegant woman appeared at the top of the impressive spiral staircase that led to the second story. She had very blond hair swept perfectly up into the latest style, and wore a form-fitting one-piece lounge outfit of deep purple. As she descended the stairs, she reminded Danni of the models who carry themselves so

19

properly erect and walk in a steadily measured pace. When she spoke, her voice was soft and breathless, an art Danni recognized from her own mother.

"Peggy, darling. How wonderful of you to come by. And this must be your friend that you told us about." She extended her delicate hand limply, with large rings gleaming on three of her fingers, toward Danni. Danni smiled and grasped her hand, noting with a tiny bit of satisfaction that the woman winced slightly as Danni perhaps squeezed just a little too hard, no doubt embedding those precious jewels into her skin.

Danni realized that her immediate reaction to this woman was intense dislike. She knew that was no excuse for behaving like she did, but after all, she was only human.

"How do you do, Mrs. Piedmont. I'm very sorry about the disappearance of your daughter."

The woman turned slightly away, and Danni noticed with ashamed satisfaction that she rubbed the fingers of her right hand as she responded, "Nancy...please call me Nancy. And I appreciate your concern." She walked towards a door on their right, indicating they should follow her into what turned out to be a gorgeous living room surrounded by floor-to-ceiling windows overlooking the beautifully manicured grounds. The room was decorated in muted tones of pale yellow, and the light that shone in the windows accented the carefully chosen pieces of furniture, including an ivory grand piano in one corner.

Peggy and Danni sat together on a comfortable couch in front of a massive stone fireplace, while Nancy busied herself with a tea service and plates of cookies that she set on a table so her guests could help themselves. The silence in the room began to grow somewhat uncomfortable, so Danni decided to plow ahead and see what she could find out -- the sooner to be done with this whole silly idea.

"Mrs. Piedmont...ah, Nancy..." she hastily corrected herself, "exactly how long has your daughter been missing?"

Nancy sat down daintily on the edge of a small chair facing them. "My *step-daughter*" she began with emphasis, "disappeared five days ago." She spoke while staring off into the gardens, as if this was a subject she would rather not talk about. It was obvious she wasn't going to offer any more information without prodding, so Danni took the initiative, again thinking how much she disliked this woman.

"Can you tell me what happened the day Jessica disappeared? Where she was last seen? Who she was last seen with? That sort of thing." Danni was proud of her discerning questions...just like Perry Mason, she told herself.

But Nancy wasn't going to cooperate. It almost seemed like she wasn't even listening. Danni was about to get testy, and put an end to this whole façade. After all, if the poor girl's parents didn't even want to cooperate, Danni decided she had more important things she could be doing with her time. Just then, another door opened and Bill Piedmont walked in. He was tall and thin, with lines of worry etched upon his tanned face. His hair was graying around the temples, and his suit hung rather loosely on his frame as if he had lost weight recently. But the thing Danni noticed most were his eyes. As they say, "the windows to the soul" or some such thing. They were deep blue and held the most sincere grief she had ever seen. Danni suddenly knew without a doubt that she would do whatever she could to help this distraught man. She felt pulled toward his feeling of tragedy so strongly she almost left her seat to run and hold his hand, to try to somehow ease the pain he so obviously felt. But thankfully before she could make a spectacle of herself, he began to speak.

"Hi. I'm Bill. Jessica left for school five days ago -- the same as she always does. At about 7:30 each morning, she walks down the driveway and meets her friend who lives next door -- Sandy -- and they are driven to school by Sandy's mom, Linda. Once in a while Nancy or I will drive them, but not often. I'm somewhat embarrassed to say, but what which my law practice, and Nancy's ...ah.... *activities*...it's just, well, more convenient for Linda to take them and pick them up." Danni saw him glance at his wife, and watched her eyes narrow and harden as a frown appeared on her face, just before she turned away once more to stare out the windows.

He continued, somberly. "Jessica usually ate lunch with Sandy and some other friends unless she had a school meeting to attend. That day, she didn't show up for lunch, and Sandy said she thought Jess had another meeting and didn't really worry about it. Then, after school, they -- Sandy and her mom -- waited for over an hour, but Jessica never showed up. They tried calling home, but we were all out, and they thought perhaps Jess had gotten a ride elsewhere -- although they were concerned since she had never done anything like that before

22

without telling them first. You see, Jess is a very sweet young lady who would never knowingly cause others to go out of their way or be worried on her account."

He rubbed the back of his neck and walked closer to them, finally sitting on the piano stool, wringing his hands in his lap. "By the time we got home and found out, I called the school and then drove over there to look for her myself -- for hours. It was getting dark, and Jessica -- she had just disappeared. I still can't believe it." He looked up at them with fresh pain in his eyes, pleading for help.

At that instant, Danni saw a flash of a place in her mind: everything was green, like a jungle almost. And a sense of water pounding, frothing -- the ocean? The image was strong and she knew instinctively it had something to do with Jessica's disappearance, but what? She decided not to say anything until she could determine more clearly what she was sensing...*feeling.*

"And what do the police say, Mr. Piedmont?" Danni asked gently.

"Call me Bill, please. They say there's no evidence of a kidnapping, and that until there is, they have to treat this as a case of a runaway child. They went into great detail to explain how many cases just like this they encounter each year. But I know my daughter, and *they don't.*" He said adamantly. "Jessica would never run away. Never. And if someone has hurt her, I swear I'll *kill them.*"

He said this with such conviction, they all believed him. Danni noticed that Nancy frowned at his words, as if all she could think of was the adverse publicity that could result from her husband's murderous plans. Suddenly, obviously wanting to put an end to the conversation, Nancy stood and looked directly at Danni.

"So, can you help? Or is this a waste of time like I told Bill already?" The blatant sarcasm in her voice was sharp, but Danni was not unaccustomed to this reaction and let it slide by for the moment, while her dislike for Nancy grew in proportion.

"I certainly can't promise anything, *Mrs. Piedmont,*" Danni answered, not wanting to be on friendly terms with this person, "but I think it seems logical to try all avenues available to learn your stepdaughter's whereabouts, *don't you agree?*" Danni smiled at Nancy's obvious discomfiture.

"Well, yes, of course. I didn't mean..." she stumbled over her words, glancing over at her husband whose own look of disgust for his wife was evident.

Bill's voice was cold and firm, and he made no effort to spare his wife's feelings as he said, "It doesn't really matter *what* you mean, Nancy. Just sit down and be quiet and let Danni alone." In response to Bill's forceful orders, Nancy lifted her chin and promptly swung on her heel, walking rapidly out of the room and slamming the door behind her.

"Don't worry about her," Bill assured them kindly, "she can't help the way she is. Really."

Danni doubted the truthfulness of this statement, but decided not to waste her time with concerns about Nancy and instead get on with the more important matter of the missing young lady.

"I guess to start with, I should look around the house, especially Jessica's room." Danni thought for a moment of how she can sometimes get very clear images from the personal effects of a particular person. "Then I'd like to meet everyone who is normally around her. I've already met Maria, but I'd like to speak to whoever else might be in contact with Jessica on a regular basis. I sometimes pick up a lot from other people, you see -- impressions, thoughts, and so on. I'd also like to meet with her friend, Sandy, and Sandy's mom, and then talk with her friends and teachers at school."

"That's quite a 'start'," Peggy chimed in. She had been quietly absorbing the whole conversation thus far. "I told you she'd be able to help, Bill."

"Now, Peggy..." Danni warned, worrying that she might be doing more harm than good for these people.

"Okay, okay already. Stop being so defensive." Peggy teased Danni, and then Bill took her hand, squeezed it gently, and whispered softly "thank you." As Bill stood there, looking into her eyes with heartfelt gratitude, Danni knew she'd give it her very best effort.

Chapter Four

Bill took Peggy and Danni on a grand tour of his home, and they poked and pried into every nook, cranny and closet. Danni sensed this was a home filled with the typical doses of love and caring mixed with some friction and discord, but nothing extraordinary. Jessica's room exuded a sense of a happy childhood, with beloved treasures and stuffed animals from years gone by placed in prominent places. There was a bulletin board on one wall with a myriad of pictures of friends, along with school awards and notices. Outside her bedroom window, there was a huge oak tree that Bill said Jessica used to climb up and play in as a younger child. His face grew soft and his eyes filled with unshed tears as he fondly remembered those precious times with his daughter.

Danni sat down on her bed, and picked up a sweater of Jessica's that had been casually laid on the bedspread. As her fingers lingered on the softness of the garment, the room around her seemed to disappear. *She felt the tang of cool salt air on her cheeks, felt the wind blowing her hair from her shoulders. She seemed to be on a hillside overlooking the ocean and behind her were rolling green fields with no visible buildings in sight.*

As fast as it appeared, the image faded and Danni blinked her eyes, finding herself sitting in Jessica's bedroom once again. Peggy and Bill were looking at Danni intensely, as it was apparent that she had experienced some sort of vision.

She replaced the sweater on the bed, and stood. For some reason, she still felt strongly about not sharing these glimpses of another place with anyone until she could get a clearer understanding of just what or where it was she was seeing, and the significance. Danni smiled at the two of them, and they seemed relieved that she was not going to relay any sort of terrible news or disquieting vision.

As she walked by the window towards the door, she noticed the gardener she had seen when they arrived. "Tell me about him," she asked Bill, pointing outside.

"That's Martin, our gardener. He and his wife Maria have been with us for over ten years now. They're like part of our family," he said fondly.

"They're married?" Peggy asked. "I never really knew -- guess I never even thought about it, actually."

"Yes, they came to us as a couple. They were referred by an associate of mine who employs Martin's brother, Jose'. We couldn't be happier with them. They've never been able to have children, and have practically adopted Jessica; Maria spoils her terribly." Bill admitted, then added, "Of course I spoil her too, I know. So I guess I shouldn't talk, right?"

"Hey, you're a terrific dad, Bill. There's nothing wrong with being good to your kid." Peggy said happily. "My parents never really had time for me, and look how I turned out. Hey, Danni -- maybe *that's* the reason I keep gaining weight. It's all my parents' fault."

Danni shook her head at Peggy's silliness. "Sure, Peggy. That's as good an excuse as any, I guess." She received a glowering look in return from her friend as they all left Jessica's bedroom and walked downstairs.

"You said you've already met Maria, and she's busy fixing lunch now, so why don't we go outside and see who's about?" Bill offered.

Danni was somehow anxious to meet Martin and see if she had any additional feelings about him since her earlier sensation of intense sadness surrounding him. She had learned that having psychic ability can be very difficult at times when you perceive things so briefly about different people and personalities. One minute you may think someone is a mass murderer, when they were only preoccupied with a compelling movie they had just seen depicting heinous crimes. Usually you can sort through the thoughts versus beliefs, but it's hard to put everything together into a complete, meaningful picture, and can be quite frustrating as well.

They found Martin near the tool shed, replacing the tools he had been using to plant the flowers earlier that morning. He nodded at Bill as they approached, then stared directly at Danni as she came closer to him.

Not noticing his gardener's unease, Bill casually introduced them. "Martin, you may remember Peggy here, and this is her friend Danni. She's come to help us try to find Jessica."

His mouth seemed to work without sound coming out for a moment, then Martin finally said, "Help? She find Jessica?" He pronounced her name "Jess-EE-ca" and looked at Danni with questioning eyes. The feeling Danni had felt earlier was replaced by a sensation of profound concern. Danni again realized that if he was as close to Jessica as Bill had said, then of course he wouldn't want to hear any bad news from a stranger like her.

"I don't know if I *can* find her, Martin, but I'm going to try." she said reassuringly. He seemed slightly disappointed or deflated, and Danni went on. "Did you see Jessica on the day she disappeared?"

"Me? Oh, no senorita. I sometimes see her in the kitchen with Maria -- I have breakfast there -- but that day I don't see her." He glanced at Bill, then continued. "Some days she no eat breakfast. I tell her she needs to eat but she no listen."

Bill smiled sadly, "I know what you mean, Martin. I'm always after her to sit down for a proper meal in the evening too, but often she's busy on the phone or over at Sandy's house. It's just her age, I guess."

Listening to this caring exchange between the two men, Danni could feel their love for Jessica. It was obvious that both cared deeply for her and would do anything to protect her from danger. After a few more words of casual conversation, they left Martin to his work and walked towards the rear of the house.

They came upon a secluded pool area surrounded by shrubs, with a cabana at the far end. It seemed to be almost Olympic size and had a professional diving board at one end.

"It looks like Jim has already been by," Bill said. Seeing the question in Danni's eyes, he explained, "That's the fellow that takes care of the pool, the spa and the entire sprinkler system on the grounds for us. He's another person who's been around for a long time. Let's see, we put in the pool about eight and a half years ago, and he started at that same time. He comes by three times a week, usually quite early, so we don't always see him. But after this many years, he's almost family too. We always invite him to our annual Christmas party, and he comes with a different beautiful girl every year. You know the type -- tall, tan and blond -- he'll probably never settle down."

In her mind, Danni was trying to keep track of the growing list of family and friends. She made the decision to begin a notebook with her thoughts and intuitions as they went along. She found herself especially anxious to see what this Jim looked like -- if he could attract all these gorgeous women. Don't get sidetracked, she admonished herself while stealing a sly glance at Peggy who was listening quietly by their side.

Relieved that no one had noticed her embarrassment, Danni's thoughts were brought back into focus as they rounded another corner and came upon a set of tennis courts that would be the envy of many tennis professionals. If she had been impressed by the size of the pool, she was totally in awe now. The law field must be pretty lucrative, she thought, then chided herself for such pettiness. She decided to ask Peggy later if all this affluence came from "old money" or "new" -- just out of curiosity, of course.

Danni hadn't noticed at first, but she now saw Nancy sitting on a bench beside the courts, one knee up while she adjusted a shoelace. Danni had to grudgingly admit that Nancy had a fabulous figure, with long tan legs and not an inch of fat to be seen. Her outfit, now that Danni looked closer, fit snugly and seemed to emphasize her "best attributes."

Sitting next to Nancy, his head practically touching hers as they talked, was a sandy haired man who appeared to be in his early thirties -- at least ten years younger than Nancy. As they approached, the man looked up first, then stood up abruptly and came to shake Bill's hand.

"Hello, sir," he said formally, pushing a lock of hair from his forehead. He carried a racket in his other hand, and had tennis balls bulging out of his side pockets.

"How are you, Brad?" Bill answered easily, glancing at his wife, who glared defiantly in his direction briefly, then resumed adjusting her shoes.

"Fine, sir. We're just about to start our lesson. Did you want to join in today?"

"No, thanks. I'm showing our guests around and have a full schedule for the rest of the day."

Danni couldn't help but notice the quick look of relief that passed over the tennis pro's young face at this news. Danni looked over at Peggy, who rolled her eyes meaningfully. As Bill said goodbye, Danni whispered to Peggy, "Glad to see a little thing like a missing stepdaughter doesn't stop Mrs. P from taking her tennis lessons."

"Yeah, although if I had a teacher who looked like that, I might be a little preoccupied myself..." Peggy began, as she shot an admiring look at Brad's retreating figure.

"Shhh." Danni admonished her, as Bill caught up to them.

Bill headed them back towards the rear entrance to the house. "That's about it as far as the tour of the place, Danni. Unfortunately, I have to be in court in an hour so I need to get going to my office. But promise me you'll keep me posted if you come up with anything, okay?" His pleading look pained her heart.

"Don't worry, I will," she answered reassuringly. She really liked this man, and felt truly sorry for his situation. "I'm going to have Peggy take me next door to the neighbor's house, and then this afternoon we'll drop by Jessica's school and see who we can talk to there. Maybe it would be a good idea for you to call and 'forewarn' these people -- what do you think?"

"No problem...I'll do it right away before I leave the house. I can't tell you how much I appreciate your help...*whatever* you can do," he said softly, then smiled sadly and walked up the stairs.

Peggy and Danni walked slowly out to the car, and sat there thinking quietly to themselves for a few minutes. Finally, Peggy said, "I don't know about you, but I think the butler did it."

It was enough to ease the seriousness of the moment, and Danni smiled in return. "I don't know, the chauffeur looks pretty guilty to me."

"What chauffeur?" Peggy asked quickly.

"I'm only kidding. Good grief." They both laughed, and Peggy started the car and headed down the long driveway.

The neighbor's house was a good quarter mile down the road, and not nearly as opulent as the Piedmont's home, but quite nice and actually more to Danni's taste. The sprawling brick and wood structure was all one story, and the surrounding woods grew practically up to the front door in wonderful, natural profusion.

As they walked up to use the old fashioned knocker on the front door, a black and white cat appeared and wound it's way around and through Danni's legs, purring loudly. This was definitely more her style, she thought again, reaching down to pet the animal.

The woman who opened the door was pretty in a natural, nurturing sort of way. She wore what looked to be her husband's old shirt over loose Levis, with sandals on her feet. "Hi, you must be Peggy and Danni. I'm Linda, Sandy's mom." She smiled warmly as she invited them into her home.

They told her who was who, and followed her through her house into the kitchen where smells of baked apples filled the air. Pots and pans hung everywhere, and the kitchen counter was covered with jars in different sizes. It was obvious that she was in the middle of canning fresh fruits, a feat Danni admitted she would never attempt, even though she loved to cook.

Wiping her hands on a towel, Linda offered them coffee and homemade cookies. "I've been just sick with worry about Jessica. I've racked my brain to try to figure out what could have happened to her. Sandy, my daughter, is her best friend. They tell each other everything. Sandy says that Jessica would have told her if she was unhappy or thinking of running away. She's just sure of it."

Danni nodded in agreement. "I think we all agree, except perhaps for the police, that this is not a case of a runaway child. Did Jessica attend all her classes that day?"

"All of the ones in the morning. The last time she was seen was in her English class, third period. It got out at 11:50 and then normally the kids all meet for lunch. But not that day."

Peggy added, "We were told how Jessica sometimes attended meetings or had other things to do at lunch. Do you know what types of meetings she went to? Or if there was one that day?"

Linda shook her head negatively. "We checked right away. Jessica had been in the Chess Club and also on the Student Council -- both of which have lunchtime meetings occasionally -- but neither had a meeting scheduled for that day." She was silent for a moment, thinking, then went on. "It's weird -- like she just disappeared or something. Although I know that's not possible. Her English classmates remember her leaving the classroom with them, and that's it. No sign of her since."

They all sat in silence for a few minutes, each with their own deep feelings. Danni was letting her mind open up to any possible thoughts that Linda might have subconsciously withheld, but found none. She emanated the vibrations of a simple, honest, spiritual person who had genuine concern for the disappearance of her daughter's best friend. There was no question about her sincerity. None at all.

"Did Jessica seem preoccupied at all that morning when you drove the kids to school? Or act different in any way?" Danni asked.

"No, I've gone over it all a thousand times in my head. She was perfectly normal in every way. Not a hint of anything wrong. Darn. I wish there *was* something I could come up with that would help." The frustration was evident in her tone.

Peggy stood and patted Linda on the back gently. "Don't worry, something will turn up -- hopefully soon. It won't do you any good to be this upset around Sandy, so try to keep yourself strong, for her sake."

"And let us know if you think of anything," Danni added. "We can talk to Sandy another time, after she gets home from school one day. I'm sure you've asked her all the same questions we would anyway."

Linda stood with them, walking towards the front door. "Yes, but maybe Danni might, you know, *pick up* on something I didn't..." she let her meaning trail off, seeing Danni's nod of encouragement.

"Sure. I'll be happy to talk to her. Just let me know when it's convenient."

They said their goodbyes and drove away down the winding road and past the Piedmont's home. "Nice lady, huh?" Peggy said, her voice raised over the wind in their ears.

"Very." Danni agreed. "But we're not getting anywhere fast, you realize, don't you?"

"Yeah." Peggy admitted despairingly.

They drove on for a few minutes, and decided, mostly at Peggy's urging, to stop for lunch and regroup. There was a wonderful little Mexican restaurant on lower State Street, with outdoor tables surrounding a beautiful tiled fountain. On the way there, Danni stopped at a drug store where she picked up a spiral notebook, ignoring Peggy's questioning look.

At the quaint little restaurant, they each ordered a jumbo margarita -- a specialty of the house – and munched on chips and salsa while Danni opened the notebook and took out a pen to begin jotting down her thoughts.

"Writing your memoirs already?" Peggy teased.

"Not a bad idea, but no, I'm making notes on our 'cast of thousands'. Everyone who had a reason to be close to Jessica, and a few who didn't."

"Like who, for instance?" she prodded.

"Okay, I may as well think out loud. Maybe you can jog my memory and add some details here and there."

Pleased to be included in this endeavor, Peggy sat forward, eagerly waiting for Danni's first observations.

"First, let's start with the parents."

"What, you seriously think they'd kidnap their own daughter?" she asked incredulously.

"No, of course not," Danni answered. "I told you I want to put down my thoughts on *everyone*, and that includes the parents, that's all."

"Oh. Okay."

"So, let's see now. Bill first. He obviously loves Jessica very, very much and is seriously concerned, to the point of threatening the lives of those responsible. He definitely feels it was a kidnapping and that his daughter would never deliberately run away." Peggy nodded her agreement, and had nothing more to add.

"Then there's *Mrs. Piedmont*." Danni said the name as if it were poison dripping off her tongue, and Peggy gave her a snide look, forcing her to start again. "Okay, *Nancy* then. Being perfectly honest, I see her as uninvolved, unloving, and uncaring. Care to add anything?"

Peggy laughed. "You mean there's more? What about self-centered, shallow and immodest?" They laughed together, then Peggy went on. "But you have to admit that it's possible she acts that way because she's, ah, *shy* or something." Seeing the doubt on Danni's face, she added defensively, "I said a *possibility*, for heaven's sake."

"Yeah, like it's possible that the Pope's Jewish." Danni remarked acidly. "Anyway, we're not really interested in what makes her behave like she does, only in her relationship with her stepdaughter. And my observation was that she doesn't seem terribly upset about the whole thing -- certainly not like a normal mother -- or even *step*mother --should be."

"Maybe she's too preoccupied with her tennis lessons," Peggy threw in with a lascivious grin.

"Don't forget the pool man, what was his name? Jim the Stud?"

"You're terrible, Danni. You should be ashamed of yourself, talking like that."

"Oh, and Nancy shouldn't be ashamed of the way she acts? Come on, now. By the way, do you know where the 'real' mother is? Lots of times they're the prime suspects in kidnapping cases, I hear."

"No dice. She died years ago. Cancer." Peggy answered between mouthfuls of spicy salsa mounded on crisp tortilla chips. "So, let's move on to the next suspect."

Taking a sip of her margarita, Danni admonished Peggy, "They're *not suspects,* Peggy. I told you..."

"All right, go ahead. I stand corrected."

"Okay now, let's see. Next we met Maria. Actually, we met her before the parents, but never mind that. She seems, oh I don't know, *deeply troubled* by Jessica's disappearance. Bill said Maria's like a second mother to his daughter...probably more like a real one, if you ask me" she muttered under her breath.

Peggy shook her head, "There you go again. But you're right: to me, Maria has always seemed like the caretaker of the household. The few times I visited their home in the past, she's always clucking around everyone, fussing with everything to make sure everyone has everything they need, and stuff. Just like a mother hen." She wiped guacamole off her lips and seemed pleased at her analysis.

"Okay, I've noted it here: 'mother hen complex'." This got Danni a pinch on the arm, which she rubbed until the pain subsided before continuing.

"Then there's Martin. I felt a lot of mixed feelings surrounding him. Sort of a sadness combined with a deep concern for Jessica. I'm putting a question mark next to him. Any thoughts you can add?"

Peggy thought about it, then said, "No, not really. I've never spoken two words to the man before. Maria is always around, but Martin stays mostly outside, hanging around in the bushes as far as I can see. He did seem upset for Jessica's disappearance, though, don't you think?"

"Sure, that was obvious. It would be really suspicious if he didn't act that way, especially if what Bill said was true and they have practically adopted Jessica since she was a baby. But I don't know, there's still something I can't quite touch about him..."

Danni gave up after a moment, knowing that there's no way to force a feeling into existence. She could only wait and absorb them when they happened.

They were served their meals, and in between bites, Danni continued writing down her notes.

"How about that Brad. In the few minutes we spent with him, I sensed a distinct limit to his brain capacity."

"Danni. What a thing to say. Why is it you pick on all the cute ones, anyway? So what if he's not an Einstein. Did you see that tush?"

Danni laughed at her friend, and nodded. "Yes, but it wasn't that much better than a lot of others I've seen."

"Well, exc-u-s-e me. I forgot for a moment that you have all the eligible men in the city running after you. Of course, one more pretty face -- or tush -- wouldn't faze you. I really don't know how you stay so uninvolved, Danni. If it was me, I'd be married with ten kids by now."

"Come on, you know you're exaggerating. You'd probably only have eight kids."

This time Danni got a swift kick in the shin from Peggy who was busily stuffing large bites of mouthwatering chicken enchilada in her mouth. Danni decided she should change the subject before she turned black and blue all over, even though she loved teasing Peggy.

"Back to my notes. I didn't feel much one way or the other about Brad's involvement where Jessica is concerned. He was so obviously concerned about being caught practically necking with Nancy in front of her husband, that I'm sure Jessica was the last thing on his mind."

Peggy shrugged, and took another bite from her plate, cheese dripping from her fork.

Danni continued thoughtfully. "But I will make a note to speak to him again, preferably away from Nancy, to see if I can pick up anything else. Then, of course there is Linda who I think we can both agree is a great person. Sweet, sincere, filled with genuine concern about Jessica. No problems there, right?"

Peggy swallowed, then agreed, "Nope. I just hope I made a good impression. I'd love her to offer me some of those canned goodies she was making."

"You have a one track mind, my dear," Danni said affectionately.

"Yep, I do." She pointed to Danni's plate. "Now, are you going to finish that taco?"

Chapter Five

Peggy and Danni spent an hour at Jessica's school later in the day, and talked with her teachers and some of her classmates who confirmed everything they had heard so far. Basically, no one knew anything other than the fact that Jessica seemed to disappear right before lunch. Danni did make another note to herself to go back to the school when there were fewer people and kids around to try to get a sense of anything that might trigger some clues.

But now, they were both getting tired and Danni suggested they call it a day. Peggy agreed to drive her home.

Because Peggy couldn't take another day off soon, Danni told her she'd go out on her own the next day. Peggy made Danni promise on her life to call with all the details the next evening, and Danni assured her she would. Danni waved goodbye to Peggy as she drove off in her little sports car, and turned towards her front door.

Without warning, an intensely unpleasant feeling hit her smack in the stomach. Danni felt sick with a premonition of personal invasion as she fumbled for her keys. It was as if she could *feel* bad vibrations coming from within her own home.

She was relieved when she opened the door to find that everything seemed to be in its place, with no obvious signs of forced entry. But still there was something definitely wrong. It seemed as if her pets sensed it also. The dogs were barking uncontrollably, the cats peeking out from behind couches and chairs. The only one who didn't seem upset was Max, the turtle, although she thought she honestly wouldn't know an upset turtle from a calm one.

She managed to settle the dogs down, and eventually her three cats came out from hiding to be stroked and reassured by her touch and calming voice. She carried one of them with her while she roamed through the house, looking for something -- she didn't know what. But the feeling didn't leave her. She was sure something or someone had invaded *her space.* Sure of it.

Finally, exhausted from the day's activities and her own uneasiness at home, she busied herself with feeding the pets and changing their water, going about things mechanically while she tried to shut her mind off.

Cooking always relaxed her, so she put on some soft jazz and inspected her cupboards to decide what to make. Since it was too much of a challenge to cook for one, she usually made enough for four and either froze the rest or gave it to Peggy, always a willing recipient. She decided on Veal Marsala, accompanied by sautéed vegetables and some freshly made pasta with pesto sauce. She opened a bottle of Chianti, and poured herself a glass, then opened a drawer to get her favorite knife.

Something made her hand stop just short of reaching in, and she looked down to see a family of scorpions scattering away from the sudden light. The glass dropped out of her hand, and she screamed, slamming the drawer shut as she ran from the kitchen.

The dogs once again came running and barking, jumping on her lap as she huddled on the couch, shaking. She was not necessarily afraid of spiders, having lived in rural areas most of her life. In fact, she tried to live *with* them, rather than *kill* them, but certainly not to this extent.

Danni made a resolution to call the exterminator first thing in the morning and have the whole house sprayed. She didn't mind sharing her property, but the bugs could have the outside, and she would get the inside.

After carefully cleaning up broken glass, sopping up spilled wine and putting away the few things she had taken out to prepare for dinner -- she had definitely lost any appetite she had earlier -- she filled a new glass with wine and took it with her to her room.

As she curled up in bed, the dogs settled down on the floor and the cats in their own special sleeping places. She sipped her wine, and thought about the day.

Missing daughters, wicked stepmothers, handsome pool men, scorpions in the kitchen: they all circled about in her head until she finally gave up, turned off the light and fell promptly to sleep.

She was floating -- almost flying -- through the myriad clouds and colors...such a peaceful, wonderful place. A destination in the distance grew closer and closer, and she strained to see what it was. Suddenly, she was there, inside some type of dark room...and she felt sadness, a painful grief. The moist heat was oppressive, and made it hard to move about. She wanted to get out. Get away. Panic began to overcome her, and she trembled uncontrollably. HELP.

Danni sat straight up in bed, blinking her eyes in the darkness. She realized she was bathed in sweat, and the blankets were tangled around her legs. Her pets were awake too, watching her with large, soulful eyes. "It's all right, guys," she told them and herself reassuringly. "It was only a bad dream, that's all." She disengaged herself from her bed and went to clean up and change into a dry nightshirt.

What was the dream about? Her fleeting memories were fading fast into that place where dreams go so swiftly upon awakening for us all. She could only remember the sensation of a hot, oppressively moist place that was confining her to the point of panic. Wondering if it could have been caused by something she ate, she remembered that she hadn't even eaten dinner that evening, so that couldn't be it. "I wonder if you can have nightmares from self-induced hunger?" she asked herself laughingly.

Deciding she had done enough thinking for one day -- and night -- she crawled back into bed and resolved to sleep the rest of the night without dreams or other interruptions.

When Danni awoke the next morning, the sun was shining and her mood was much improved. She took care of the dogs, the cats, and the turtle, then called the bug man who promised to be by shortly. She settled for a glass of orange juice, not wanting to chance finding any more surprise visitors in her kitchen drawers.

When the bug man arrived, he seemed quite surprised that the scorpions had settled in her kitchen drawer. It's not the usual place where they are found, he told her simply. In fact, in all of his days of exterminating, this was a first. It was almost as if someone had put them in there on purpose, he mused.

Something about that last statement made Danni feel very unsettled, and the strange feeling she had felt the night before returned. Then, rationalizing that she was just upset by this whole spider situation, she put her feelings aside and proceeded with making sure the pets were all outside for the day so they wouldn't be affected by the strong spray being used inside her house.

She went to the garage and carefully opened the door, still looking for bugs where she was used to seeing them. But seeing none, she proceeded to get in her car, a 1967 Mach I Mustang -- cherry red with black interior, and back it out. She loved her car, and had kept

47

very good care of it since buying it new, replacing the engine once a few years ago. It used a little more gas than the newer models, but she didn't care. She loved the way it handled, and the powerful engine purring under the hood.

As Danni arrived at the Piedmont's home, she noticed a police car parked in the driveway. She was sitting there trying to decide if she should wait or come back later, when the front door opened and Bill came out, talking with an officer. Then both of them looked her way. Damn. Now she would have to get out and go through the humiliation of one more person who would no doubt find it ridiculous to believe in such a thing as psychic ability. Most people are unwilling to even consider it a possibility.

Danni sighed heavily as she got out, resolved not to let the officer's anticipated remarks bother her. She starred down at the ground as she walked over to where they were standing. She was certainly not prepared for the shock she received when she looked up into the face of the man in the dark blue uniform. This was a face different from any she had ever seen -- or so it seemed. He was not traditionally handsome at all, but yet Danni felt so attracted to him immediately that she felt a blush travel up her cheeks clear to her forehead. He had the most beautiful eyes, a pale green in color, and the smile that slowly spread on his face made her heart skip a beat. His thick, dark black hair shone in the sunlight as he removed his hat and took a step in her direction.

Danni quickly glanced down at her own disheveled appearance. She never really paid much attention to what she wore these days, darn it. Her jeans were old and worn, though they had shrunk and fit her long legs snugly, she admitted. And she had thrown on a bulky old green sweater that had seen better days, not ever dreaming she would be meeting a man to die for today.

Bill, who no doubt thought Danni had lost her senses (which indeed she had, she admitted ruefully to herself), cleared his throat and introduced them. "Detective Reghetti, this is Danni -- oh, I'm sorry Danni, I don't know your last name."

"Speranza" she said softly, accepting his hand as he gently reached out to hold hers. The warmth seemed to creep up her arm and explode in her heart, and she could feel it pounding so hard she was sure the thumping was visible from the outside of her sweater.

"Italian?" he asked in a voice that sounded like a melody to her.

"What? Oh, yes...yes. My father was Italian. From Genoa."

As he released her hand (regrettably, she thought), he smiled again, and Danni felt like she would faint any minute. "Ah, then we should get along fine. My family is from Milan, so we are both Northerners. I'm glad you're not Sicilian -- I would have had to teach you the error of your ways, as my grandfather would have said," he teased.

Bill again interrupted, making a coughing gesture to let them know he was still standing there. "I'm just leaving for the office, Danni. Was there anything you needed from me before I go?"

She tore her eyes away from her dream man long enough to smile at Bill and answer, "No, that's fine. I thought I'd just poke around for a while, if that's okay. Is your wife around?" she asked, hoping against hope that she wasn't.

"No, she's off on one of her escapades today," he answered, despondently. "Did you need to speak with her?"

"No!" Danni answered a bit too abruptly, and noticed the officer's eyebrows rise with a question in his eyes at her vehemence. "I mean, uh, no thanks. I can always talk to her another time."

"Good, then I'll see you later. Feel free to call me if you need me." Bill said as he walked towards his car.

Danni gazed back up at the officer. He was still studying her intently and the warmth returned under his scrutiny. "Detective ... Reghetti, was it?"

"Call me Luke. It's really 'Luca', but no one in America can understand that, so I've changed it to just plain Luke."

Just plain Luke sounded wonderful to her. "Okay, but you have to call me Danni. Short for Danniella -- Danniella Luisa Celestina Speranza -- actually."

He grinned at her with the most incredible smile, making Danni almost ache inside. "Wow. Now I know you're Italian. I thought I was the only one with so many names. Luca Luigi Marcello Reghetti."

They laughed together, and it seemed so natural and right. Danni wondered if he felt the same way. She didn't have to wonder for long.

"I know this is short notice, but would you be interested in dinner tonight?" he asked hopefully.

"I'd love it, but only if you let me cook."

"You'd better watch out," he said huskily, "if you cook as good as you look, I may ask you to marry me."

"You'd better watch out yourself. I might just say yes."

He took both her hands in his, then leaned forward and she closed her eyes expectantly. She felt like one of the leading ladies in a love story, waiting for a kiss as she raised her lips to his. But to her surprise, and embarrassment, she felt his soft kiss on one cheek, then the other -- not her lips -- and she opened her eyes to see him smiling that same way that made her melt before him. What was happening to her? Was it possible to fall in love so fast? Was this the proverbial "love at first sight" everyone talked about?

"I have to go now, but I'll see you tonight, Danni."

She nodded, and gave him her address, telling him to come over any time after 6:00, hoping he wouldn't make her wait a minute longer than necessary.

As he drove away in his patrol car, he waved goodbye, and Danni stood there on the porch like an idiot waving and watching him until his car turned a corner and she could no longer see him.

"Now I know I've flipped for sure," she said to herself. "Wait until Peggy hears about this." Thinking of Peggy made her remember what she was there for in the first place. Taking a deep breath, and shaking her head to get back to the business at hand, she decided to take a walk around the house and see if any new prospects showed up to be interviewed.

Danni looked for Martin, but didn't see him. It was entirely possible he could be anywhere on the vast property. There was no telling, and she soon gave up looking for him. The pool area was again deserted, and the tennis courts seemed empty too. Then, just as she was about to head up to the house, Danni saw the unmistakable shape of Brad as he bounded around the side of the house. He spotted her at the same moment, and looked as if he was going to turn around to leave, so she called out to him and waved.

He shrugged and waved back, then walked over to where she was standing.

"Hi," he said simply. "I came by to pick up some rackets that need adjusting."

Danni wondered briefly why he felt he had to explain his presence to her. "Hello. We met yesterday."

"Yeah, I remember. Nancy, er, Mrs. Piedmont said you were some kind of mind reader or something -- trying to find the kid." His voice held a subtle hint of laughter and obvious disbelief in her capabilities.

"Well, *Mrs. Piedmont* was somewhat correct." She deliberately stressed the 'Mrs.', hopeful but doubtful that the hint would penetrate his thick skull. "I *am* trying to find her daughter. But I'm not a mind reader, I just have what some people refer to as psychic capabilities."

He seemed confused as he tried to figure out the difference -- Danni was not really sure what it was either, but wanted to make him think she did. He seemed to give up after a moment, then asked, "Oh, well, didja find her yet?"

"No, not yet. But I'd like to ask you a few questions, if you don't mind."

"Me? Sure. Do I get a reward if I help you find her or anything?"

"I'm sure Mrs. Piedmont would be *most generous* in showing her gratitude to you if you can be of help." she assured him smoothly.

"Oh, yeah...right," his answered, his averted gaze telling her he knew Danni was aware of his intentions as far as his tennis student was concerned.

"Anyway, do you see Jessica around often?"

"Not much. She hates tennis. Mostly likes to study and run around with her friends, I guess. She's a real pain in the ass sometimes, though, according to Nan, er, Mrs. Piedmont."

It was obvious he was warming to the discussion, so Danni encouraged him. "Oh, really?"

"Yeah. She told me once that she was considering one of them boarding schools for the kid just to put her someplace where she would behave. I guess, from what I heard, that the old man, ah, Mr. Piedmont, nixed that idea though. He's got a real soft spot for the kid."

"Not like Mrs. Piedmont, eh?"

"What? Oh, I didn't say that, now. Don't go putting words in my mouth. Mrs. P is just real busy with *things*, you know...she has lots of stuff to take care of all the time, and the kid just gets in the way, from where I see it. Besides, she would'a probably liked being in a fancy school for rich kids. I know I would have. Horseback riding and shit like that..."

"Possibly," Danni said non-commitedly.

"Anyway, Mrs. P is a nice lady. I don't know why she stays with her old man. Probably feels sorry for him I guess. But she sure isn't happy with him. Who would be? A guy like that, always fightin' people, putting people in jail." Seeing the surprise on her face, he went on. "I have a right to my opinion. I don't give a damn for him. But I like her." He winked and smiled broadly.

"I bet you do," she thought to herself. Then she responded out loud, "Thanks for your time, Brad. If you think of anything else, please let me know. Mrs. Piedmont has my number."

Still looking confused and unsure of where Danni stood in this household, Brad smiled halfheartedly and walked away.

Danni shook her head in wonder at what any woman could possibly see in a man like that. She took out her notebook and jotted down some thoughts, including the fact that she found Brad to be shallow, not very bright, and with a one-track mind as far as Mrs. Piedmont was concerned. However, she had to admit she didn't seem to feel anything sinister or malicious about him, and made a notation about that also.

She shut her book and turned to walk back to the house in the hope of finding Maria to ask her some questions while she was alone and not influenced by others. She nearly bumped right into a man who came around the corner of the house suddenly, his arms full of sprinkler pipe and fixtures.

"Oh, sorry." she said as she backed up and steadied herself.

"No problem." he answered abruptly and then walked off, his head down, toward a storage shed without giving her a chance to say another word.

Danni decided that this must be Jim, the pool/spa/sprinkler man. She watched him walk away and acknowledged that he was attractive, all right, but somehow she felt it was only skin-deep. Her exposure to Jim was so fleeting that she didn't have any kind of impression one way or the other about him. She opened her notebook and made a note to corner Jim sometime soon, then realized it might not be easy to get through to some of these people, even if it might mean helping to find Jessica.

In the house, she followed her nose to the big, roomy kitchen where she found Maria humming a melancholy melody and stirring a steaming pot on the stove while gazing wistfully out the window. Danni cleared her throat to get Maria's attention, and succeeded in scaring the woman. Maria jumped as she turned to face Danni, her hand on her heart.

"Oh, senorita, I didn't hear you come in." She put the spoon down and wiped her hands on her apron, a look of genuine concern falling over her worn face. "Do you find anything to help my Jessie?"

Danni was immediately sorry once again that she ever agreed to get mixed up in this mess. She wanted nothing more than to be able to say "Yes, sure. I've found her and she'll be home any minute." But, instead she had to admit sadly, "No, Maria, I have not. Perhaps it would be better if we just let the proper authorities handle this whole thing?"

Maria's look tore at Danni's heart. "Oh no, please, senorita Daniella...you must not give up. My poor little Jessie is out there somewhere, and she needs your help."

Danni went over to hug Maria, and tried to comfort her with her words. "Okay, Maria, I promise I'll try to help. I promise."

They stayed huddled together for a few moments, each deep in troubled thought about the whereabouts of Jessica. Then Danni motioned for Maria to sit down with her at the kitchen table to talk.

"Maria, even though people say I have a gift of inner sight, well, I believe everyone has the same ability." Danni noticed Maria's look of doubt, then continued. "You must open your mind and tell me if you have sensed anything strange recently. Has anyone acted differently than usual? Done or said something that seemed not quite right to you? Think, Maria, think." Danni held Maria's hand, urging the woman to cooperate, but it was obvious Maria could not or would not admit to any ability to see beyond the obvious.

"No, senorita, I do not know what you say. I cannot tell you anything to help." Then Maria pulled her hands away, and wrung them in her lap. "But, Heaven forgive me, I do not like the Senora." Maria hung her head in embarrassment at her bold declaration against the wife of her employer.

Danni smiled, then agreed with her sympathetically. "Don't feel bad, I totally agree with you. She's about the most cold-hearted, self-centered individual I've met in a long time. I don't know what Bill sees in her, but then love works in mysterious ways, they say."

"Sí, but the way she treats little Jessie -- as if she is dirt -- it is not right." Maria complained, shaking her head left and right.

"Is she truly abusive to her, Maria?" Danni asked with serious concern.

57

"She does not *hit* her, if this is what you mean. But she is *muy malo*...always complaining about my little Jessie -- and right in front of her too. Poor baby sometimes cries herself to sleep because of her...I know this to be true."

Danni felt the tug at her heart at the imagination of what it must have been like for the little girl to live under the same roof with such a woman. She tried to temper her anger as she asked, "Doesn't Bill do anything about it? He obviously loves Jessica dearly, and I'm surprised he puts up with it."

"Oh, she is smart, that one. She says nothing in front of him. She knows better. She waits until he is gone, and then she picks on her, *pobrecita*. I think maybe she is *glad* that my Jessie is gone, *Dios Mio*." She crossed herself at the terrible thought that this might be true.

Danni shuttered also. Even a stepmother shouldn't behave that way. If she disliked the girl so much, she shouldn't have ever married Bill. But, nevertheless, the marriage had obviously happened and there was nothing that could be done to undo the past. All that Danni could do would be to try and find Jessica, and then perhaps see if she could talk with Bill to enlighten him as to his wife's behavior towards his daughter. What a mess.

Maria talked for a while about what a special child Jessica was, and how much she and Martin loved her. Danni smiled at the fond memories Maria described -- all the happy times they had shared together.

Then, smelling her stew about to burn on the stove, Maria hurried over to stir it and began clucking about needing to get back to her dinner preparations. Danni took the hint, deciding it was time to be on her way. After all, she reminded herself with a grin, she was having company tonight -- wonderful, delightful company.

Danni said goodbye to Maria and drove down the long driveway, again not seeing anyone prowling amongst the trees and shrubs that were abundant around the property.

She headed for her favorite market on upper State Street, mentally planning what her menu would be for this evening. It would have to be something special, but not overwhelming. She didn't want to overdo it on their first 'date', so she decided on one of her favorite, but most basic recipes for homemade lasagna, accompanied by a fresh green salad and crispy french bread heavily laden with her own garlic butter.

Chapter Six

She only needed to pick up a couple of things since she kept most everything stocked at home, so she arrived in plenty of time to prepare for the evening. Her pets were anxiously awaiting her return when she got home that evening after being outside all day long. They jumped up, barked and meowed while she got their food ready, then they settled down. Confident that all of her "bug" problems were taken care of, she jumped into the shower before starting her preparations for dinner.

She hummed happily to one of her favorite jazz albums in the background while she put together the fresh ingredients for her meat sauce and set it to simmer while she mixed the semolina flour, eggs and water for the homemade noodles she would use. Sipping from a glass of cold Pinot Grigio, she thought again of how strange yet wonderful her meeting with Luke had been.

She stopped suddenly, and worried to herself, "What if it was only a fluke? What if he comes over tonight and all the magic from our earlier meeting is gone? Anything is possible with me lately." Then she shrugged her shoulders and told herself it was no use worrying about it -- if that happened, well -- it happened. They would have a pleasant evening -- she would cut it short as possible -- and that would be that.

But maybe, just maybe -- she allowed herself to dream of the possibilities if it wasn't a fluke. The warm feeling she had felt when he had touched her returned, and she found herself imagining something other than dough under her fingertips as she kneaded the mixture to its correct consistency. Her lascivious thoughts were interrupted abruptly when her doorbell rang and she realized it was probably Luke. He was early and she wasn't even ready. She was wearing only the t-shirt she had slipped on after stepping out of the shower. Her hair was still wet, combed straight back from her face -- with no makeup. Good grief. Was it possible she could look any worse?

But her fears disappeared when she opened the door shyly, hiding as best she could from his delighted eyes as he took in her appearance. "I'm glad to see we're not 'dressing' for dinner. Personally, I hate being uncomfortable. Mmm..mmm. What smells so good? No, don't tell me. It's something with a meat sauce, and lots of garlic and basil. Whatever it is, I'll love it." He marched past her and walked towards the kitchen, sniffing with appreciation.

Danni closed the door and stood watching him, her heart pounding. She took in his lean but muscular frame, and admired the view from the 'rear'. It was definitely no fluke, she told herself with glee. 'My, oh my, oh my -- am I in trouble this time,' she thought silently.

She joined him in the kitchen where he had found a spoon and was tasting her sauce. "Fantastic. So when do you want to get married, tonight? Or shall we wait until tomorrow?" He laughed as she opened her mouth to protest. "And don't look at me like that or I'm liable to forget I'm a gentleman and then we'll both be sorry." His eyes traveled hungrily down her body and he stared with obvious appreciation at her long shapely legs in clear view beneath her short shirt.

Watching the route his eyes were taking, she gasped, "Ah, let me run in and change. I'll just be a minute." She dashed out of the kitchen and ran down the hall towards her bedroom.

"Don't change on my behalf. I told you, I like what you're wearing just fine." he yelled after her with laughter in his voice.

Luke hit his forehead with the palm of his hand, as if trying to snap out of this crazy reverie he was spinning around in. He was renowned by both family and friends as the guy who probably would never settle down. With his good looks, attractive girls were always swarming around him. He never went on more than one or two dates with any one woman, always finding them shallow and dull and so he moved on to the next. He had pretty much decided his family and friends were right about him, that is, until he met Danni. Or rather, Daniella Luisa Celestina Speranza to his Luca Luigi Marcello Reghetti! It had to be fate, he thought to himself as he sat down and began petting the various dogs and cats that were vying for his attention.

When Danni returned, she was wearing a simple sleeveless chemise in her favorite shade of lavender, and comfortable sandals on her feet. She had foregone putting on any makeup except for a light blush and some pale lipstick. After all, this was the way she liked to be: au natural. See if he liked it -- she hoped he would.

Luke smiled when she entered the room, his approval of her appearance evident in his eyes. He had poured himself a glass of wine, and handed her glass to her for a toast. "To us, bella. To our future, our children, and our long life together." His gaze settled steadily on hers.

Danni couldn't help but smile at the thought of such a prediction coming true with this wonderful man, and took her sip of wine without dissention. "To us", she agreed, smiling.

Luke sat in the kitchen and watched her while she finished preparing their meal. They carried on a comfortable and easy conversation -- almost as if they had known each other for years. She couldn't get over how at ease she felt with him -- it was uncanny. Not since Sam had she met someone who felt so *right*...and yet there was something different about her feelings for Luke. Something deeper and more *solid.* As if two halves of a whole had finally come together and they fit perfectly.

Over dinner Danni brought up the subject of Jessica, and Luke told her everything he knew, which unfortunately wan't much more than Danni had already surmised. He explained the police department's normal procedure in cases like this and sadly said that until there was evidence of a kidnapping, the rule was to treat it like a runaway case. At Danni's exasperated response to this, he quoted statistics that supported the runaway probability, but Danni was not convinced.

"Can you honestly say that you believe Jessica ran away? Forget about police department procedure for a moment, Luke, and tell me the truth. What do you really believe?" She looked into his eyes searchingly, and he frowned, then answered softly.

"Truthfully? I think you're on to something. From what everyone says, she's not the type of girl to run away. But what can I do? My Captain won't let me spend any more time on the case unless something breaks to change things as they now stand."

Sensing the frustration in his voice, Danni relented a little and reached out to take his hand. "I know, and I'm sorry to push you like that. It's just that this case has touched me so much . I feel so badly and wish I could help -- it's very frustrating."

They were quiet for a moment, holding hands across the small candlelit table in front of her fireplace. The music played soothingly in the background, and everything would have been perfect, Danni told herself, if it wasn't for her deep concern about Jessica. Every minute that went by she worried about what might be happening to Jessica now. Was she being treated well? Was she even alive? Her thoughts drifted...

The flash of bright light as the door opened hurt her eyes and she backed away from it. She felt the familiar fear return and

retreated into the farthest corner of the room -- away from THEM.
After a moment, the door closed again and she smelled the non-
disguisable fragrance of a familiar favorite dish...hot, spicy chili...then
the blackness returned.

"Danni? Are you all right?" Luke grasped her hand tightly, and rubbed her arm with his other hand.

"Chili." Danni focused on Luke's face, the concern evident in his eyes. She felt...she was almost sure now...that Jessica was indeed alive and that the glimpses were an indication of where she was being kept. "Oh, yes, I'm okay. Just thinking..."

"You had a vision, didn't you?" he asked softly, timidly.

She hesitated, afraid to admit her ability to this wonderful man. What if he laughed? Or worse, what if he scorned her for her silly beliefs? She told herself she may as well get it over with, and find out now before this relationship went any farther.

"Yes. I don't know what it means yet, but I felt something. It was somewhere strange..."

"Bill told me about your being a psychic, Danni. I want you to know I think it's a great gift -- and you may be a big help in finding Jessica."

Danni looked at him with obvious surprise, and he smiled, then continued. "I have to admit I used to be a real skeptic when it came to stuff like this before, but since joining the force, I've seen too many instances of things that are just plain unexplainable. Not to mention the fact that we've used psychics ourselves a couple of times and had a pretty good success rate. So, who can say what's possible and what's not." He looked at her tenderly. "Certainly not me."

Relief was evident on her face as she beamed at him across the table. "I know what you mean. My mom thinks I'm making the whole thing up, and to be honest, sometimes I wonder about it myself. But then things happen that I *knew* about beforehand, or I know what someone's thinking, or about their past -- it's strange, and scary -- but it *is* real, at least for me."

"I know, bella, I know. And I think it's just one more thing that makes you so special -- so different. You should only be proud and happy that you can help others in this way."

When he put it like that, she felt so pleased and happy. It meant so much to her to have him understand how she felt, and even more so that he liked her that way.

After dinner, Luke helped her clean up the dishes, complimenting her sincerely on her great cooking -- almost as good as his own grandmother - his 'nonna' -- he had said. She was thrilled and very, very flattered. She was again struck by the realization that she hadn't felt this way about anyone ever before -- not even Sam.

As she put away the last of the dishes, she turned and asked him softly, "What's happening here -- with us, I mean?"

Luke drew her into his arms and held her so close she could feel his heart beating next to hers.

"We finally found each other, my love." He lowered his lips to caress her forehead ever so lightly. "I know it's strange that it happened so fast -- I've been thinking about it all day too. But I'm also a believer in fate -- or destiny -- and bella, this is it, I think."

"Fate," she repeated slowly, gazing into his eyes with wonder.

Then the magic of the moment carried them away and his lips met hers for a soft, lingering kiss. She trembled in his arms as the raw emotion she was feeling threatened to overcome her senses. She prayed the moment would never end -- that they could stay close like this, in each other's arms, forever and ever.

Luke led her over to sit on the couch in front of the fireplace. Two of her cats, curled up nearby, opened their eyes to stare at them, then stretched and went back to sleep.

Danni lay in Luke's arms with the fire warming them for what seemed like hours. They spoke of their respective pasts until they felt they knew every detail about each other. She shyly told him about her nickname and how she got it, and he laughed as he said, "I love it. Princess. I know, I'll call you my 'Psychic Princess'. It's perfect."

She joined in his laughter, caught up in the happiness he had brought her. "But what shall I call you? Do you have a nickname, Luke?"

His face grew serious as he answered, sincerely, "Whatever you call me -- and whenever -- I'll answer, my love." This time his kiss was filled with an urgency that invaded both of their bodies to the core. They strained against each other, their hands touching, feeling, and memorizing every inch of the other's body.

Danni realized, vaguely, that she wanted nothing more than to give herself to this man -- now -- this very moment. Since Sam she had not been truly intimate with anyone else, and her sudden need to make love to Luke was tremendously powerful. She whimpered in frustration at the clothing that separated them. Luke moaned as he fought the burning desire building within him.

His hands groped for hers, and he suddenly held them both still.

"No, bellissima, not like this. First you must become my wife. Then we will make love until the dawn of time."

Danni saw the futility of arguing with him as she recognized the conviction in his voice and face. In a way, she was pleased at his response. And anyway, she was sure he wanted her as much, if not more, than she did him.

Danni thought dreamily to herself that a normal person would never believe such a thing could happen – meet and fall in love in the same day. But she felt a bond so incredibly strong, Danni wondered if perhaps they had lived other lives together.

They sat up and she snuggled into his embrace. "I believe you said something earlier this evening that sounded like a proposal to me - - does that offer still stand?"

He smiled and her heart melted, sending a delicious tingling sensation down her spine. "You know it does, my little Psychic Princess. But I should talk to your mother first, and you must meet my family also."

Danni groaned with feigned impatience, "Good grief, Luke. It'll be next year before we do all that." She ran her fingers sensuously down his chest, stopping just short of his belt.

Now it was Luke who fought for control. "No it won't, I promise. We'll show everyone the quickest whirlwind romance they ever saw."

Danni giggled and they spent the next hours making plans for their future -- a future that seemed much brighter to both of them now.

Chapter Seven

Luke was good to his word. The next few days flew by in a daze as he introduced Danni to his huge family and all his closest friends. Danni had him meet Peggy, who cried tears of happiness at her friend's good fortune. She was not the least bit surprised at the spontaneity of it all, and delighted in helping take care of most of the wedding details.

They decided on a small service at beautiful Butterfly Beach. They made arrangements to be married by a friend of Bill's who was a judge. Danni's mother gave her approval by phone from the Italian Riviera, saying she would see them at Christmas when she planned a world cruise with her latest lover.

Even with all the excitement of their marriage, Luke and Danni both still devoted countless hours to Jessica's disappearance. They knew without saying it aloud that there would be no honeymoon until Jessica was found. Bill tried to change their minds, but was secretly relieved when they refused.

By the day of their wedding, five days after they met, Danni had completely reorganized her notebook. Although she still had no clear idea of where her notes led her, it was at least a start. Luke, meanwhile, spearheaded a community effort at posting missing person posters with Jessica's picture on them during his off-hours. Together, they worked tirelessly to end the search for the missing girl.

Danni had not had any further psychic insights relating to Jessica since her first evening with Luke. Peggy thought she was justifiably preoccupied with getting married, and Danni agreed that might be the reason.

In addition to the wedding and reception plans, Danni had to reorganize her house to accommodate all of Luke's belongings, though he didn't really have that much. He had been living the life of a typical bachelor in a studio apartment since leaving home at eighteen, and didn't really have much he cared to keep. Danni was also glad that he didn't have the typical macho attitude about moving in with her...as far as they both were concerned, that was the only thing that made sense.

As Peggy adjusted the lacy veil complementing Danni's simple but elegantly beautiful wedding dress, she had tears of joy in her eyes. "You look so beautiful -- just like a real princess. I swear your mom was right for once when she gave you that nickname."

Danni laughed and hugged her friend happily. "Thanks, Peg -- for everything. You'll always be a part of our family."

"Oh yeah, I can just see that," Peggy teased. "I somehow don't think Luke would appreciate me around for the next few weeks."

"Don't be silly," Danni answered with mock sincerity. "Of course he would. But *I* wouldn't." They both giggled, then Danni went on, "Tell you what -- we'll have you over for dinner real soon -- I promise."

"If I believed that, I'd probably end up losing ten pounds by the time it happened." Peggy countered playfully. "Hey -- another diet breakthrough idea. I love it!"

On the day of the wedding, it was sunny and mild, with not a cloud in the sky. The wedding – held on a nearly deserted stretch of beach with the ocean waves lapping near their feet -- was simple and short, attended only by Peggy and Luke's parents. They had a small reception at Danni's home afterward, and before long, they were alone at last.

Luke took her gently into his arms. "My mother and father love you, bella. As does nonna. She couldn't say enough about your antipasti. She's so happy to have someone to pass down all her famous Italian recipes to."

Danni laughed and kissed her new husband. "And I love all of them too, darling. You're very lucky to have such a wonderful family. As you know, my mother is a little on the strange side..."

He grinned and hugged her tight, then picked her up to carry her toward the bedroom. "Ah, but perhaps that's what makes you so different from everyone else. I wouldn't have you any other way..."

She kissed his neck and felt his body tense with longing. "Did you say something about 'having me'?"

He laid her down gently in bed, and it was late the next afternoon before they left it.

Chapter Eight

Since they got married on a Saturday, Luke and Danni did allow themselves one day -- Sunday -- as a pseudo-honeymoon until they could take a real one. They walked on the beach for hours, sharing their mutual love for the ocean and it's ever-changing uniqueness. The sun shined down on them as they lay entwined on the warm sand until they couldn't stand it any longer and raced back up to the house for solitude and sweet love.

Then on Monday it was back to work for Luke, and back to Jessica's search for Danni. It had now been two full weeks since her disappearance, and no ransom notes or other indication of a kidnapping had materialized. Luke again apologized to Danni for not being able to do more from his position with the police, but Danni assured him he was doing plenty to help, and not to worry.

Luke had become immediately possessive of Danni since they had met, and now that they were married, he was extremely uneasy about her continuing her activities at the Piedmont home by herself. Peggy was unable to get off work to accompany Danni, but Danni finally convinced Luke that she was in no danger -- there were always plenty of people around the house -- it was not like she would be there all alone.

He reluctantly gave in, but made her promise to call him every few hours to let him know she was okay. Danni wasn't used to this type of behavior -- she had been terribly independent for so long -- but secretly she admitted to herself that she loved knowing he cared so much about her and her welfare.

This time, as Danni drove up the long driveway towards the house, she thought she saw Martin by some rose bushes off to one side of the property. But when she pulled to a stop, she saw that either she had been mistaken, or he had left the area where he had been standing just moments before. She frowned as she felt a familiar sense of something not being quite right, then shook it off as she grabbed her notebook and set off to see who she could find.

Bill greeted her with sincere appreciation at her effort to help find Jessica, and when she asked if Jim was around, he told her where to find him. Danni could tell that Bill had been suffering tremendous strain from worrying about his daughter, and was barely able to cope at this point. She wanted to say something to console him, or even encourage him, but couldn't think of the words. She sighed and turned away, anxious to look for more clues.

Danni approached Jim from behind as he worked on the pool filter, and she was almost up even with him when he spun around, a wrench raised instinctively in his hand.

"Oh. I'm sorry if I startled you." Danni said as she took a step back from his menacing stance.

Jim lowered his hand, and visibly relaxed somewhat when he saw who it was. "You shouldn't sneak up on people that way. Could get hurt." He turned back to his work then, obviously not anxious to participate in a conversation at that time.

But Danni was not one to give up so easily. She walked around the equipment until she was facing Jim over the top of the filter. "I'd like to ask you a few questions, if you don't mind."

Jim finished tightening a piece of pipe, then looked up at her with narrowed eyes. "What type of questions?"

Danni felt a strange combination of pain and hatred emanating from this man. It was so strong at that moment that she almost forgot what she was there to ask. She sensed he had had a terribly unhappy childhood -- filled with unspeakable misery at every turn. Jim seemed to realize what she was reading from his eyes, so he tore his glance away from hers and resumed his work in earnest.

"Oh, uh, about Jessica. I'm trying to help Mr. and Mrs. Piedmont find their daughter." She wondered why she felt compelled to explain herself to his man, but she did notice a look of compassion pass quickly over his face before he blocked it out completely.

"Sorry I can't help. I don't know anything about it."

He had finished whatever repairs he was making and was picking up his tools, about to go off to his next project. Danni felt compelled to say something quick before he could once more get away without giving any definite answers to her questions.

"Wait. It's possible you know more than you think. Just tell me if you saw Jessica often. Who she was with, that sort of thing. Anything you can think of might help," she pleaded.

Apparently the look of sincere determination on her face was his undoing, and he set his toolbox down and stared at her, his hands on his hips.

"Jessica is a good kid, okay? She's not like most kids her age, into drugs and stuff. She's smart. And, well, *good*."

He ran his hand through his wavy brown hair, and Danni was once again struck by his rugged good looks. No wonder every woman he met was bowled over. Of course his particular type of handsomeness didn't appeal to Danni -- it was too obvious -- too up front. She preferred her sweet Luke and his perfect body...perfect for her, anyway.

But again, she felt there was something dark and foreboding deep inside of Jim. She could almost *touch* it, *feel* it. And then, as she reached out and touched his arm, she suddenly saw it all. *The beatings, the screaming, the crying, the pleading for mercy*. This man had been subjected to such horrors as a child that it made Danni gasp. She found her hand flying involuntarily up to her face in shock. Jim looked at her, the cold suspicion of all others reappearing in his eyes.

77

"I've gotta go now. I've got a lot of work to do." He said as he hurriedly picked up his toolbox and strode off towards the garage.

Danni didn't try to stop him. She couldn't have even if she had wanted to, she knew instinctively. She was still trying to recover from the unbelievable feelings she had felt about Jim. Could a childhood like that lead someone to do something equally violent in manhood? You heard about things like that happening all the time. Danni shuddered at the thought of a young girl being at the mercy of someone like Jim. But yet, she reminded herself, he had sounded so normal, even *nice*, when he was describing Jessica to her.

It was all too confusing to figure out right at that moment, and Danni sat down on a pool lounge chair to make copious notes on her experience with Jim for later review. Maybe if she discussed it with Luke, he would know what it could all mean, if anything. After all, Luke dealt with deranged people all the time -- he should know if anyone would.

Danni was so engrossed in her note-taking that she didn't notice that the door to the pool house was ajar until she heard a woman's laughter coming from within. Danni put her pen and notebook away and stood up, and just before she went to investigate she stopped as she heard Brad's deep voice coming from inside the same place. "Oh my God," she thought disgustedly, "Brad and Nancy are together in the pool house." She couldn't believe the audacity of the woman to behave so outrageously right on her own property. What if her husband were to come out here now?

But even as she was thinking this, she heard Bill's voice from right behind her.

"Hello Danni." He held out his hand to her, a sad smile on his face.

"Oh, ah, hi Bill." Danni responded nervously as she glanced quickly at the open pool house door.

Seeing her concern, Bill took her by the arm and led her away towards the house. "It's okay, Danni. I've known all about it for quite some time, now. It's Nancy's way of getting back at me for being gone all of the time, I think."

"But, how can she...?" Danni began, disbelief evident in her expression.

Bill shook his head, and said kindly, "It doesn't matter anymore. Really. I was going to get around to asking her for a divorce, and then Jessica...." he stumbled over his words, a tear running down his drawn cheek.

Danni felt her heart in her throat -- she felt so sorry for this man. First he loses his daughter, and now this? It was too much for a person to bear, she thought sadly.

But Bill wiped away his tears and smiled bravely, escorting her through the rear door to the house. "Please, don't worry about it. What's important is getting Jessica back -- nothing else."

As they walked back into the house and headed for the library, Danni agreed, "You're right, absolutely. But please let me know if there is ever anything Luke and I can do to help."

"You're already doing more than I could have ever hoped for with your efforts in trying to find Jessie." He took her over to sit in a window seat area that overlooked the beautiful gardens outside. "This was...*is*...one of Jessica's favorite places to sit and read. Perhaps you can...*feel* something here."

"Thank you. I'll try." Danni said sincerely.

"I have to leave to get back to the office now. You have my number there if..." he let the words remain unspoken, dropping his hands to his sides with a sigh and walking away, closing the door quietly behind him.

Danni sat for a moment in thought about the many strange events evolving here in this troubled household. She gazed out the window and saw why Jessica would love sitting in that particular place. It was very cozy and the view was peaceful and beautiful. She tucked her legs up underneath her and leaned back against the comfortable pillows. Then, feeling a slight lump behind her, she pulled out a small paperback book from between two of the cushions and glanced at the title: *A Summer of Hope*. She flipped the pages absentmindedly, seeing that it was a novel about young love and stolen kisses, and she smiled. So Jessica was at that age, eh? Danni clearly remembered going through that painful time of emotional growth.

Suddenly, her hands froze on the pages of the book. A crystal clear image came into view in her inner mind.

She was sitting in the same window seat. It was raining outside. A fire was burning in the fireplace. She shivered when she heard loud voices from the other side of the door. She laid the book aside, then stood and walked ever so slowly towards the door. As if in slow motion, her hand reached out to turn the knob. The door opened slowly, just a crack. Just enough for her to see the couple standing there. They were so close, yet seemed so far away...a blurred image. The man was shaking the woman, yelling at her. The woman was crying hysterically, pounding on his chest with her fists, her hair a tangled mess.

As if alerted to her presence, they turned towards the door where she stood, a silent witness to their anger. The man took one step -- then another -- towards her. She could feel her heart beating wildly.

Danni felt the coldness -- oh so cold -- in her chest. As if her heart was frozen solid. And then she felt the hate -- pure, hot hatred -- she hated them both so much. She wished, yes, she did wish, that they were <u>dead</u>. Both of them.

The book dropped from Danni's hands onto the floor, and she snapped out of her reverie. Poor Jessica. Was this what she had experienced while living in this house? Danni could not be sure of the validity of her visions, but knew that she had never felt such hatred. She shuddered as she tried to clarify in her mind exactly who the two people in the hallway had been. But it was no use. They had appeared to be in some kind of a haze, and even if it had been a clearer image, Danni felt sure she wouldn't have recognized them.

But what had they done to little Jessica when they discovered her standing in the doorway? Had they hurt her? Or threatened her? Danni shook her head in frustration at the questions that were prompted by her 'mini-visions'.

Finally, giving up on her efforts to clarify her glimpse into the past, Danni said a silent prayer, once again asking for divine protection for the young girl they were all so desperately trying to find. She went back to her notebook and had just finished writing about this latest episode when the door to the library swung open and Luke walked in, a look of quick relief descending over his face.

"Luke. Why are you here? Has something happened? Have you found Jessica?" Danni asked with hopefulness in her voice as she rushed into his open arms.

He kissed her forehead, then shook his head as he answered, "No, no news about Jessica, honey. I'm sorry." Then his look of sadness changed to one of mock severity. "But you -- you promised to call me and it's been over four hours. I was worried so I came by, and then no one knew where you were, and Bill was gone."

She laughed as she interrupted him, touching her fingers to his lips. "Sh...h.h., my darling. I'm here and I'm fine. You mustn't worry so much. After all, I *did* manage to keep out of trouble -- most of the time anyway -- before I had the good fortune of meeting you." She smiled warmly.

He hugged her tight, his arms encircling her possessively, she fit there so perfectly. "Yeah, well, things are different now. Not to mention the fact that you're nosing around in the middle of a missing person's case -- you've never been in *that* situation before, have you?" he demanded smugly.

She had to admit she hadn't, and anyway she loved the secure feel of his strong arms around her so she didn't dare argue.

Danni finally convinced Luke that she was OK, and promised reluctantly to be home within the hour. Luke got in his car to go back to work -- he had been assigned to a case involving the theft of computer chips from a research and development company in Goleta, and his boss was on him big time for a swift and conclusive end to the case.

Danni watched him drive away, and was about to turn to go back into the house when she again saw Martin at the edge of the garden. She waved and started down the steps to go talk to him, then stopped suddenly as she saw him quickly retreat into the trees. How odd, she thought. Was he deliberately trying to avoid speaking to her? She convinced herself it was unlikely. After all, Martin and Maria both loved Jessica like their own daughter -- you'd think he'd want to do whatever he could to help find her -- but then anything was possible with this group, she thought ruefully. She decided to go and ask Maria about her husband's strange behavior -- she'd certainly have time to do that and still be home in an hour as she had promised.

Danni went into the kitchen but didn't see Maria anywhere. She knew that Maria and Martin lived in the caretaker's cottage on the outer edge of the property and thought briefly of walking out there to see if they were there, then decided against it. She was already intruding into these people's lives enough as it was, and her question about Martin's behavior could wait -- it certainly wouldn't mean the difference in finding Jessica, she assured herself firmly.

She decided to give up for the day and was walking towards the front door when she came to a halt at the bottom of the staircase and looked up. A strong feeling came over her, pulling her go up to Jessica's room once again, by herself this time. Glancing at her watch to make sure she had plenty of time, she made her way quietly up the stairs, feeling almost like an intruder in this big, unhappy household. Maria was out somewhere, Bill was at his office, Nancy and Brad were probably still outside in the pool house fooling around, she thought with disgust, and she was here all alone. It was a little disconcerting, yet she felt compelled to go into the room, and do so *right now*.

Everything seemed to be the same as it had been the last time she had been in the room with Bill and Peggy. She was drawn to the window where she gazed out at the big oak tree that Jessica used to climb on. Danni stepped even closer to the window, and placed her palms upon the panes.

Psychic Princess: Admirable Avocation

Suddenly the tree before her eyes dissolved and faded away and another image began to appear, slowly coming into focus. She was again on a hilltop overlooking the ocean and could feel the tangy salt air misting against her skin. As if in slow motion, she turned and took in the rolling green hills, the tall grass blowing gently in the wind. She willed herself to move forward, although it seemed more like floating than walking. Then, as she came to the top of a small hill, she looked down and saw what looked like a small town or village. There were no streets, only dirt roads, heavily rutted from wheels pulled through vestiges of muddy days gone by. The feeling that was pulling her forward was getting stronger now, and she moved forward down the hill. She was approaching the outer edge of the village, when she vaguely made out a handwritten wooden signpost and strained her eyes to read the words printed there. They were so very worn it was difficult to make out. It looked like 'Castillo de...' she willed herself to stand taller to see the last two words. They seemed to be either 'San Carlos' or 'San Carmello'. It was so very difficult to be sure. Her head was beginning to pound from the effort she was expending. She felt faint, weak.

"Senorita Daniella. Esta bien?" Maria's worried voice reached Danni's ears just as she felt herself grasping the window frame to keep from falling. Then Maria's arms were around her, helping her to regain her balance.

"Oh, thank you, Maria. I guess I was feeling a little faint there for a moment."

"Come, you must sit down." Maria guided Danni gently over to the bed.

Danni willingly agreed to sit still as Maria clucked over her like a mother hen -- reminding her of Peggy's appropriate description. It gave her a chance to quickly memorize her latest vision so she wouldn't forget anything before she got a chance to write it all down.

After a bit, Danni assured Maria that she was okay and they both descended the stairs to go into the kitchen for a cup of tea that Maria insisted Danni have before leaving. Danni waited until Maria was seated next to her, sipping her own cup of tea, then asked her, "Maria, I wanted to ask you about your husband."

"Si, senorita?" Maria looked up, a curious expression on her face.

"Yes, you see it seems as if he might be, well, sort of avoiding me lately." She rushed on before Maria's obvious objections could be voiced. "No, listen. Twice now I've seen him on the grounds and the last time, I know he saw me wave at him. But then he disappears before I can catch up to him. Do you have any idea why?"

Maria stood up and took her teacup to the counter, her back to Danni. "No, senorita. I am sure you are mistaken. My husband would not do such a thing. I am sure of it. Perhaps he did not really see you. Do you want me to go and find him for you now?"

Maria's look of innocent confusion at Danni's accusation made her feel silly for even thinking such a thing. "No, that's okay. I'm really just grasping at straws, as they say. Trying to talk to everyone as much as possible until I can maybe figure out what could have happened to Jessica. I'm afraid I'm not doing a very good job, though."

This last statement made Maria rush to Danni's side and place her hand upon Danni's shoulder. There were tears in Maria's eyes as she pleaded, "Please do not say such things, senorita Daniella. You are *an angel* to try to help us as you are doing."

Maria's words softened Danni's doubts about her abilities once again. She just *had* to keep trying as long as Jessica was missing, she decided.

Chapter Nine

Danni arrived home in plenty of time to meet her husband's 'curfew', as she thought of it with a smile. She set about getting the food out for her hungry pets, talking to them lovingly while they wound around her legs with enthusiasm. She knew having two dogs and three cats was a bit much -- not to mention her turtle. But Luke had taken it all in stride and the pets seemed to adore him immediately. She even found herself getting a little jealous at first when their affection was so easily transferred from her to him. Then they seemed to even out their attention between both Luke and Danni, and all was fine once again.

She suddenly remembered that she had forgotten to bring in the mail, and opened the door, the two dogs following excitedly. She just wanted to get to the mailbox before it got any darker, and then she'd finish feeding them, she decided. Her mailbox was at the end of her driveway along with several others for adjacent properties. She was about to open the door to her mailbox when her two dogs began barking and jumping hysterically at her. Thinking they were overly hungry, she pushed them aside and started to reach in to get her mail when suddenly she heard it.

She jumped back just as the rattlesnake snapped it's deadly jaws in the air where her hand had just been, missing it by mere inches. Her heart was beating wildly now, as she searched wildly for a rock or some other weapon to use on the creature. She was used to snakes on her property -- after all she had lived in the Faith Ranch area of Santa Bella for years. But rattlesnakes were something else altogether. And how did this one get in her mailbox, she wondered. She knew that snakes liked dark places, but she also knew they didn't have hands to open mailbox doors with. Just as she saw a large rock on the ground, the snake slowly slithered out of her mailbox and disappeared into the nearby bushes. Her dogs continued to bark in serious protection of their beloved master, and she pulled them back, not wanting them to get bitten instead of herself.

Danni checked the box thoroughly before retrieving her mail, and made a mental note to be more careful in the future. She couldn't take much more excitement in her life, she thought ruefully. If only my damn psychic ability worked for me too, these things wouldn't happen. She decided suddenly not to tell her husband about this – he would only worry needlessly. She trod on back to her house, both dogs right behind her, and calmed down while reading a long letter from her mother before fixing dinner.

Her harrowing experience with the snake all but forgotten, she lavished seasonings on a small roast and put it in the oven next to a pan of small red potatoes drizzled with olive oil and tossed with sage and fresh parsley. It was wonderful having someone else to cook for now besides just herself, even though nothing had ever gone to waste before with Peggy as an permanent leftover eater. She sliced some Roma tomatoes and put them aside to marinade in a homemade vinegar, mustard and olive oil dressing, then picked out a bottle of Merlot to complement their meal.

Satisfied that her initial preparations for dinner were well under way, she decided to go over her notes so far and see what sense she might make of them. She passed her art studio on the way to the living room and frowned again forlornly at her most recent half-finished sculpture. She didn't know when she would get a chance to complete it now. But certainly her search for Jessica was much more important.

Just then the phone rang, and Danni smiled as she went to pick it up, knowing instinctively that it was her friend Peggy calling. Peggy had made it a habit to call almost every evening and catch up on the latest news about Danni's search for Jessica. Peggy was desperately unhappy that she couldn't be more active in helping Danni look for clues, but her boss had asked her to work extra hours to get ready for the Christmas season. She hated it, but she needed the money so grudgingly agreed to his wishes.

Danni found herself not going into too much detail about her psychic glimpses with Peggy. Poor Peg was overly optimistic when it came to Danni's capabilities, and she would only make things more complicated. So, it was easier to be vague and tell Peggy only that she was doing her best to help find Jessica, and leave it at that. Of course, she had to talk about something, so Danni kept Peggy updated on the various conversations she was having with the cast of thousands at the Piedmont home.

As a result of her overactive imagination, Peggy had already decided that Nancy was definitely the guilty one, having knocked off the young girl as a twisted form of revenge against her husband before running away with the tennis instructor. It was for reasons just like this that Danni was glad she kept the rest of her thoughts and intuitions to herself.

After finally convincing Peggy that nothing else was new, Danni hung up and went to settle down on an overstuffed loveseat near a window overlooking her garden and the ocean beyond. She pulled out her pen and opened her notebook, then entered the details of her most recent vision. As she looked out at the waves crashing on the shore, she recalled the sensations she had experienced in Jessica's room that day. The pounding surf, the rolling hills, the tall grass waving in the wind, the secluded village... Where was it all leading, she wondered? What did it all mean?

She was studying all the various notes she had accumulated on the different people involved in the Piedmont household when Luke arrived home. He walked over to her swiftly and picked her up, twirling her around in his arms. "M..mm..mm. I love married life. I've never been so eager to get home before," he crooned lovingly in her ear.

Danni hugged him back and lavished kisses all over his face and neck. "Same here. If I would have known being a wife was so much fun, I would have gotten married ages ago."

Luke held her away from him, and narrowed his eyes accusingly. "Wait just a minute, there. Are you saying you would have married someone else besides me?"

"No, silly. *Fate* would have just seen to it that I met you sooner, that's all." She leaned into his embrace even closer, enjoying the feel of his strong body next to hers.

They spent the next half hour talking over their respective day, up to the point where Luke had come to find Danni at the Piedmont's house.

"I still say you don't need to be quite so protective of me, my love," Danni admonished him gently while stroking his brow with loving fingers.

"I can't help myself, princess. You've become an integral part of my life now and I don't know what I'd ever do if anything happened to you." He held her tightly, running his lips down her cheek to her neck.

"I have a feeling that the only thing that's going to happen to me right now is something wonderful…mmm..mm…and sensual…"

She groaned in delight as he caressed her, lowering her to the floor where they made love with frantic abandon, their pets watching with disinterest from a respectful distance across the room.

It was several hours later when they had finished eating Danni's delicious meal and were sitting contentedly in front of the fireplace. This was becoming one of their favorite places in the cozy house, besides the bedroom, of course. Danni loved to have a fire burning in the big brick fireplace on most days of the year, except the few when it was unseasonably hot. Living so near to the ocean, a fire took the chill out of the moist sea air on foggy mornings and late evenings.

Danni reached for her notebook, Luke's arm casually wrapped around her shoulders. "Mind if I have a look?" he asked.

"No, not at all. As a matter of fact, I wanted to go over everything with you anyway to see if you have any different impressions or ideas than me."

Luke nodded and sat quietly reading through her pages of notes, at times frowning and at other moments stopping to look off into the distance with a look of intense concentration on his face. Danni waited silently, staring into the fire with her own thoughts circling in her mind.

Then Luke turned to her and asked, "Of all the people that you've talked to -- Bill, Nancy, Maria, Martin, Jim and Brad -- who do you have the strongest *negative suspicions* about?*"

Danni thought for a second, then said, "I don't know if I'd call them *suspicions* exactly, but I guess I would have to say...Jim."

"I agree." Luke stated with conviction. "You've written your own observations with a personal slant towards your psychic insights about these people, and what you've said about Jim points towards the one individual with the most question marks, in my opinion."

"But do you think he could seriously be involved with Jessica's disappearance? I mean, just because he's had a rough life and I picked up bad vibrations about him, it doesn't automatically make him the prime suspect, does it?"

He squeezed her gently, and smiled. "Of course not, bella. I just find in my line of work that your first instincts are generally the correct ones, and you should go with them. I think I'll do a little digging of my own into his background. And that Brad too, while I'm at it. I've got a friend at the department who owes me a few favors and he can get just about any information you'd ever want to know about a person for me. I'll get on it first thing tomorrow morning."

Danni nodded, thinking she could do a little more checking on her own, but deciding not to bother Luke with her plans -- he would be sure to complain about her continued involvement.

Before setting the notebook aside, Luke scanned the last few pages one more time, looking slightly pensive.

"What is it, sweetheart?" Danni asked.

"I'm not sure. Just your note about the words on the wooden sign you saw in your vision. 'Castillo de San Carlos', or 'San Carmello', you wrote."

Danni struggled to remember clearly what the sign had said, but her efforts only succeeded in bringing back the feeling of exhaustion she had experienced earlier. It was no use. "I'm sorry, I couldn't really say for sure what it said. Do you think it's important?"

"I don't know, bella. I don't know."

Chapter Ten

As Luke kissed her goodbye the following morning, he told Danni to behave herself today and stay at home. He was adamant that there was nothing more to be learned at the Piedmont home, and he wanted to do some checking around himself. He smiled as he told her to go work on her sculpture, since he wanted to have a finished piece to show his parents what a talented artist he had married. Danni nodded noncommittally, and waved to him as he drove off.

As soon as he was gone from view, she rushed to the phone and dialed the Piedmont's home number, hoping to catch Bill at home before he left for the office. She was relieved when she heard his voice at the other end of the line.

"Hello, Bill? This is Danni. I wondered if you could give me some information."

"Sure, Danni. What do you need?"

"Well, I'd like to go and see Jim, at his office. You know, to get an idea of where he works, and so on."

She knew it sounded odd, and didn't want to seem as if she was casting suspicion strictly on Jim. Bill's voice did sound a little confused when he answered, "Uh, of course. If you think it would be of help. But the only address I have for him is the one we send his Christmas invitation to -- I'm not really sure if it's his home or his office, or both. He may work from home, I mean."

"That would be fine, Bill." She assured him, trying to sound nonchalant. She waited while he went to fetch the address, and wrote it down on a slip of paper. "I'll talk to you later, then. I don't think I'll be by the house today. I'm sort of taking care of some other business, if you know what I mean."

Bill didn't know, but was too exhausted from worry about Jessica to think much about Danni's perplexing attitude. He said goodbye and went off to get ready for work.

Danni threw on a jacket over her light blouse and jeans and grabbed her purse and keys, throwing kisses to her pets as she left. The address that Bill had given her was on Milpas Street, and it took her only ten minutes to drive up to the old, Spanish style building and find a parking place. This was the type of building that housed several businesses, some shops, and usually had some personal residences upstairs. The numbers were painted on the peeling stucco in faded red paint, and it took Danni a few moments to find the one she was looking for on the second floor in the back.

As she walked up the worn slab stairs, the hair on the back of her neck began to twitch and she wondered if what she was doing was such a wise idea. After all, she could be walking into a murderer's lair, for all she knew. Then, chiding herself for being overly dramatic, she marched resolutely up to the large wooden door and knocked loudly three times. No one answered, and she tried twice more to no avail.

Feeling frustrated at coming this far with no results, she timidly tried the handle of the door, turning it slowly to the left, then right. She gasped in surprise when the door clicked open and she released the handle, letting it swing inwards by itself with an eerie creaking complaint.

She couldn't swallow, her throat was so dry, and she felt frozen to the spot where she stood. Her eyes took in the spartan appearance of the one room office/studio. It was obvious that this was indeed where Jim lived and worked from. Various plumbing tools and pipes of all sizes were stacked near one wall, and an unmade bed strewn with newspapers was against the adjacent wall.

Deciding she was in for a dime, in for a dollar, Danni took two tiny steps into the room and let her eyes continue their search. She wasn't even sure what she was looking for. She just needed to see -- and *feel* -- whatever she could about this unhappy, pain-filled man.

Her eyes were suddenly drawn to a dark corner of the room near what was apparently his closet. Next to piles of clothes, some hung haphazardly, Danni saw a collection of photographs pinned to the wall. Willing herself to be brave, she walked closer, until she could see that they were all of the same little girl in different poses. All of the pictures were taken when the girl had been a young teenager, perhaps between the age of eleven and fourteen or so.

Danni's eyes traveled to one large picture in particular that had one corner slightly bent. She reached to unpin the photo from the wall and it fell into her hands. Carefully, she studied it up close. The child was plain, but attractive in a waifish kind of way, and looked almost haunted if you looked deeply enough into her eyes. Finally, Danni turned the picture over and read the writing scrawled in pencil there: "Lucy, two days before her death, December 14, 1988."

Danni dropped the picture as if it had turned to a burning hot coal, searing her fingertips. Her death. The young girl in the picture had died? Why did Jim have her pictures on his wall? Her imagination leaped to the possibility that perhaps this child was a former victim of his foul play. She had read about murderers who kept pictures of their victims pasted on their walls or in albums, almost as if to gloat at what they had done.

Danni suddenly became terrified of being caught in this terrible place by Jim...or anyone else for that matter. She rushed out the door, leaving it ajar in her haste. The picture of the young girl lay bent on the floor where Danni had dropped it, partially hidden beneath a pair of worn work shoes.

Danni drove the short distance to the public beach parking lot on Cabrillo Blvd. and pulled in with a peal of burning tire rubber. She screeched to a stop and turned off her motor, then sat gripping the steering wheel tightly while she tried to calm down. What had she done? Whatever could have made her do such a foolish thing? Luke would be furious if he found out about her dangerous escapade. She vowed silently to herself not to tell him, that's all. After all, she hadn't been caught, and she was alright, so there was no sense in upsetting him unduly.

Convinced that she was doing the right thing, she calmed down enough to think through the accusations she had hastily made about Jim and his collection of photographs. Was she jumping to conclusions just because she felt uneasy about the man? The pictures could have been of anyone -- perhaps a friend, or relative. On the other hand, she thought as she remembered the strange way he had acted the few times she had seen him, perhaps the young girl *was* someone else, and he had been involved in her death.

Shaking her head to clear it of the confusing thoughts she was having, she got out of her car and walked down to the water's edge. This was where she always came when she needed to refresh herself, the ocean held a special place in her life. She couldn't imagine ever living away from it.

An hour later, feeling drained and strangely empty of feelings, Danni headed back to her car and home. All she wanted to do was have her husband's strong arms around her, comforting her. She just didn't want to think anymore. "Sorry, Jessica, but I just can't," she whispered to the wind.

Chapter Eleven

When Luke came home that evening, he called to Danni from the front door, but heard no answer. A look of worry crossed his face as he went from room to room, finally finding her fast asleep on top of their bed. The larger of the two dogs lay at the foot of the bed on the floor, and the smaller one had curled up next to her legs. The three cats were huddled together near her head, as if protecting her from unknown dangers.

"What a great bunch of security guards you guys make," he whispered to them as he knelt down to stare at his wife's lovely face. He noticed a look of faint worry upon her brow and reached out to smooth away her cares with loving tenderness. It almost scared him how much he loved her. Was it possible his love could continue to grow even more through the years? Would he be able to handle it if it did?

Yes, he told himself. With Danni by my side I can handle anything, anywhere, anytime. She stirred beneath his touch, and her eyes flickered open, a sleepy smile curving her soft, inviting lips. Slowly, he bent to kiss her ever so lightly, as if afraid she would break.

"Hi," she whispered softly. "I guess I fell asleep."

"I guess you did, little one. You've been doing too much lately," he said with concern evident in his voice.

'If you only knew,' she thought to herself guiltily. Aloud she said, "I'm sorry I don't have dinner ready. Let me get up and I'll start it right away."

He pushed her back down gently, and winked. "No, tonight it's my treat. I can cook too, you know."

"You can?" she asked in amazement.

Pretending to be annoyed at her surprise, he responded, "Certainly. Why, there are any number of delicious dishes that I know how to prepare. Now let's see -- what would you prefer, hamburgers or hot dogs?"

They laughed together at his silliness, and she said, "A hot dog sounds wonderful. I haven't had one in years. They're some in the freezer, along with some buns."

"I know. I checked it out already. You never know when you might not be home and I could be ravenous. A man has to be prepared at all times."

He blew her a kiss then and made her promise to stay in bed, saying he would serve her there. "After all, a princess deserves nothing but the best, you know."

She threw a pillow at him as he rushed out the door towards the kitchen.

Later, with mustard and catsup spills on their shirts and hands, they finished the last of their sodas while sitting cross-legged on top of the bed. "Now this is what I call true gourmet food," Danni teased him.

"Do you want another? I could fix you one more," he offered as he reached to take her empty paper plate and napkin from her and headed for the door.

"No thanks. I couldn't eat another bite. You really are a good cook, honey. And here I thought I just married you for your cute buns," she teased playfully.

He glanced down at his behind as he stepped through the doorway, and then smirked. "Not bad, eh? But don't worry -- you're pretty well endowed yourself."

This time she did manage to hit him with another pillow before he dodged it, and then she followed him into the kitchen carrying their soda cans. The dogs got up and pounded after them, thinking it might be their turn to be fed.

Luke relented and poured some more kibble in their bowls, as he said, "By the way, I got a basic background on our friend Jim today."

Danni sat down to listen. "Really? What did you find out?"

"Well, among other things, he never finished high school. He dropped out at sixteen and joined the merchant marines. His parents split up when he was a kid, and he and his sisters lived with his old man -- not the most pleasant personality from what I read."

He saw the question in her eyes, and went on after sitting down across from her. "Apparently his old man had a severe drinking problem. He had a long list of arrests for drunken disorder and stuff like that. Even served two years later on for a small-time liquor store burglary." He shook his head, sadly. "Sort of fits right in with what you sensed about him, doesn't it? Jim couldn't have had a very happy childhood with a dad like that, and no mom to speak of."

"I guess you're right," Danni agreed reluctantly as she thought back to the pictures on Jim's wall, and shivered involuntarily.

"Are you okay?" Luke asked.

She smiled, then said, "Yes, I'm okay. It's just sad to hear about a family like that with no love, no direction in their lives -- it's such a pity."

"Yeah." Luke was silent for a moment, then went on. "But in any case, Jim seems to have kept his nose clean -- at least so far. He had a few minor skirmishes in the service, but nothing major. He was a bit of a troublemaker at times, but received a medal for service beyond the line of duty in Vietnam. So, I guess the guy can't be all bad."

"I'm sure you're right," Danni agreed. But how could she tell him her suspicions about the pictures on Jim's wall without admitting that she had gone to his room today? After mulling it over quickly, she decided perhaps there was nothing to it after all. Luke had checked him out, and if he wasn't worried about Jim, then why should she be? Still, those pictures stayed in the back of her head...the little girl's melancholy face staring out at her with those big, sad eyes.

Luke then told her that his friend was still checking into Brad's background -- he had to conduct his investigation on his lunch hour since it wasn't an official police request -- yet.

As they lay down to go to sleep that night, Danni snuggled up close into Luke's embrace, and sighed. They were both quiet with their own thoughts.

Danni was still thinking about Jim and the pictures on his wall. Then she thought back to her glimpse of the strange place near the ocean, the village, the sign.

Luke was preoccupied with his own mental errand wanderings: the words on the sign Danni had seen -- San Carlos, San Carmello -- the observations she had made about the various people at Jessica's home. Jessica, poor little Jessica...

Chapter Twelve

The morning dawned clear and bright, and Luke and Danni awoke feeling refreshed and much less preoccupied than the evening before. Luke set off for the department with silent determination to do some more checking on his own. He decided not to share his intuitions with Danni, not just yet. His years of training made him want to have some solid evidence -- or at least something more than pure conjecture -- to back him up before he made a statement of his beliefs.

Danni decided to step away from the search for Jessica for a few hours and get back to her sculpture. She felt it might help her to get her mind off things for a while...perhaps give her a fresh outlook that could help her see things more clearly. At least that's the excuse she used with herself as she went about preparing to work with renewed effort.

She was in deep concentration, trying to get the piece to look just the way she wanted it, when the phone rang two hours later. Wiping her hands on a clay-covered cloth, she went to answer it.

"Hello?"

"Danni." She heard the tension in Luke's voice from just the one word.

"Luke, what is it?" she knew immediately that something had happened. Something important about Jessica.

"We've got a note. A ransom note."

The awesome words rang in her ears. She couldn't believe it. Finally, they had positive proof that Jessica's case was a kidnapping. In a way she was relieved, but then just as suddenly she was deeply concerned.

"Do you think she's okay, Luke? I mean, you know how these things work. They wouldn't hurt her now if they're trying to get a ransom for her, would they?" Danni's voice held the built-up emotion she had been storing since she first got involved in the case.

Luke listened with empathy tearing at his heart, wanting to assure his love that everything would be all right. But he knew he couldn't lie to her that way. It would be worse in the end if things *didn't* turn out all right.

"I'm afraid there's just no way to tell, bella. We've seen all kinds of things happen here at the department over the years. Just when you think you can read some of these cases, they twist and turn and come out all different than you would have ever thought, I'm sorry."

"Me too. Have you talked to Bill yet?"

"Yes, we went to his office and talked to him personally. The note was sent to his home and his wife called us right away. She seemed to be quite upset over it."

"Either that or she was putting on another one of her good acts," Danni said petulantly.

"Now, Danni," Luke began.

"I know, I know. I'm sorry. Now is not the time for recriminations against a selfish, stupid stepmother."

He smiled a little at his wife's unbelievable honesty. It must be nice to be able to speak so sincerely, if caustically, about others. But he knew she would only speak the truth as she saw it, and admired her for it.

"Anyway," he went on, "it seems to be a legitimate note. We've had our lab analyze it. We're taking it seriously."

Danni shook her head in ignorance at the ways in which the police department worked. She wouldn't have even thought to suggest that the note might be a fraud. Good thing it was her husband, and not her, working for the department.

"So what's next?" she asked him anxiously.

"Well, now comes the difficult, time-consuming procedure of trying to track down the source of the paper, the typewriter, and so on. There were no fingerprints, of course, and it had been hand-delivered to their mailbox sometime early this morning." He answered her next question before she could ask it. "And no, no one saw the person who dropped it off. We already checked with everyone."

"Luke, what does the note say? What are they demanding?"

Luke wasn't supposed to share that information with anyone outside of the department, not even his wife. But he knew instinctively that she would find out somehow anyway, so he told her. "It says -- in rather crude English, by the way -- that she is being held where we won't find her, that we shouldn't even try to, and that they want a million dollars cash to be raised for delivery within forty-eight hours."

"Forty-eight hours. So soon? Can you possibly find them in that time?" Danni wondered skeptically.

Luke confirmed her concern. "It's doubtful, honey. But we're going to give it our best shot. The Captain has assigned ten of us to the case now that we have something tangible to go on. The kidnappers said in their note that they'll be contacting us again with instructions about the drop-off. We hope to have some leads before that time comes. In the meantime, you won't be seeing much of me, I'm afraid. We're all putting in double duty on this one."

The admiration and love showed in her voice as she responded, "Don't worry about me, sweetheart. You just find Jessica, and I'll be the happiest wife around." She smiled, then grew serious once again.

Suddenly Danni asked, "Luke, do you think I could see the note? Just for a moment? I might be able to get something from it."

109

He cut her off abruptly. "Now Danni, I don't think that's such a good idea." He also knew it was strictly against the rules. He shouldn't have even told her about it to begin with, and now she wanted to look at it, for Heaven's sake.

"Look, *Detective Reghetti*, you said yourself that your department uses psychics all the time to solve crimes. What's so different about this one?" she demanded.

"First of all, we don't use psychics *all the time*, just *some* of the time. And second, you're my wife and I don't want you involved in this anymore -- it could be very dangerous. And thirdly…"

"Those are all just silly excuses." she interrupted him sharply. "I'll be down to see you as soon as I change. Goodbye."

She hung up before he could speak again, and she didn't answer the phone when it started ringing a minute later.

Chapter Thirteen

Luke's Italian heritage was reflected clearly in his furious demeanor when Danni strode purposefully into the department on Anapamu Street, just as naturally as if she belonged there. In fact, Danni had only been there once before, when Luke had taken her in to meet the guys he worked with before their marriage, and she wasn't too sure where to find him. It turned out he was waiting for her.

She gulped when she saw the look on his face, not sure yet of how far she could push this new husband of hers, but then she pressed on resolutely. After all, if there was a chance she could help them find Jessica before the kidnappers' time ran out, all the more reason for her to try.

Two other officers were standing behind Luke as she stepped up to him, her chin held high. She glimpsed their slightly smirking looks, going first from her then back to Luke. Ignoring them, she said firmly, "I'm here to see the note."

Luke's voice was as cold as ice, and just as thin. "I told you not to come down here, Danni." He grabbed her by the arm and led her away from the other men's ears and eyes. "Damn it, you should have listened to me."

"Damn it yourself, Luke. This is serious business and I'm here to help. Now stop being so melodramatic and give me the note."

The Captain had come out from his office upon hearing the commotion, and walked up in time to hear Danni's last statement. He looked at Luke inquisitively.

Luke stumbled over his words, his head hung low in embarrassment over his wife's audacity. "Ah, sir, you see, my wife here is, well, she's sort of psychic sometimes, and well, she thought that maybe..."

"So, Reghetti, what are you waiting for? If she can help, let's let her take a look."

The surprise was evident on Luke's face. He turned and saw Danni's look of satisfaction quickly turn to concern as she realized what she had just done. Even she knew better than to humiliate a man in front of his superior. But what was done, was done, and now she just wanted to get on with it.

They walked into a small cubicle where a man was studying a piece of paper under a bright light and had what looked like a jeweler's loupe firmly pressed against his eye.

"Bitterman, let this young lady have a quick look at the note." The Captain's order left no question as to the outcome and everyone moved aside for Danni to approach the table. Before she reached it, she was handed some thin plastic gloves much like the ones surgeons wear and instructed to be careful not to smudge any of the marks on the note.

You could have heard a pin drop in the room as Danni slowly read the note, then sat down to look at it closer. The words had been typed using what appeared to be a very old typewriter with some of the letters missing, and others were barely readable. The paper was plain white, the type you could pick up just about anywhere, but Danni noticed a stain of some kind in one corner.

Her eyes focused on that particular area of the paper, ignoring the words printed above. She brought her fingers closer and closer to the page, then touched it lightly, while closing her eyes.

He had sworn violently as his hot coffee splashed on his hand and on the corner of the paper. He was dark...very dark...not only his skin but the color of his hair was almost pitch black. There were pockmarks on his forehead and cheeks, deep ones left from childhood, and a scar left a thin raised welt across his face from his ear to his throat. She tried in vain to see his eyes, the eyes of the man who she knew held the secret to Jessica's whereabouts. It was no use, but she could smell him. She was overwhelmed by the stink of filth and dirt and sweat all mixed together. It made her begin to choke and cough.

Danni was pulled out of the chair and handed a glass of water to stop her coughing fit, and Luke was there holding her, murmuring into her ear. He still loved her, she thought with relief, then realized they were all waiting to hear what she had seen.

"I saw him..."

"Who?" the men all chorused simultaneously.

"The man who wrote the note, I think," she said weakly. She went on to describe her vision as clearly as she could while one of the other officers made notes of everything she said.

"Did you get a name?" Luke asked gently.

"A name? Let me think." she again closed her eyes in concentration, hesitantly but determined to go back to the dark place where she had joined with the thoughts of the dark man in the strange place.

It came to her suddenly and clearly. "Fernandez." she said sharply. "I think, Luis. Yes. His name is Luis Fernandez."

Chapter Fourteen

Jim swore under his breath as he came to the top of the stairs and saw that his door was wide open. He quickly scanned the room and saw that nothing was missing, and then reminded himself that he had nothing of value to steal, so he wasn't terribly surprised.

He took off his jacket and threw it on his bed, then shoved some of the newspapers onto the floor and sat down. He rubbed his forehead, trying in vain to ease the throbbing headache he had. The headaches were coming more frequently now, and lasted for days sometimes. The doctors had told him it was because of an injury he had suffered in Vietnam. Well, he had brought back a lot more than headaches from that experience, he thought to himself angrily.

He didn't know when the last time was that he had gotten a full night's sleep without the terrible, thrashing nightmares he suffered. On the few occasions when he used to have a girlfriend and sleep over at her house, she would become intensely afraid of him after one of his harrowing nighttime experiences. Apparently, he screamed some pretty terrifying things and usually ended up on the floor from his wild lashing out at unknown enemies.

He was still massaging his temples when he glanced over and noticed the picture on the floor. He stood and went over to pick it up, holding it in his big hands and staring at it for several minutes. Then he looked up, and over to the open door. He was going to have to do something soon...very soon...

Nancy stretched one long, elegant, tanned leg out from beneath the mounds of bubbles in her bathtub, and sighed contentedly. She was remembering her afternoon of torrid lovemaking with Brad -- right there in her own bedroom. She wondered fleetingly if Bill even cared anymore when or where or whom she saw or what she did with them. It certainly didn't seem like it. They had both realized not long after getting married that theirs was not a marriage made in heaven. More like Hell, she thought to herself as her leg slipped back down into the warm soapy water.

Now Brad, on the other hand...she squirmed as she thought of his hands and mouth moving over every inch of her body. He would, and had, done just about everything with her. What a lover. Then she smiled wistfully and thought silently, "if only he had more than a pea brain in his head, he's be perfect. Oh, and a few million in the bank wouldn't hurt, either."

But she was no fool, that's for sure, and she was not about to give up a good thing with Bill as long as she had it. And since she was sure Bill knew about Brad, and didn't even care, it seemed to her that she could do whatever she pleased without recrimination.

Such a deal.

Things would really be perfect if the kid never showed back up, Nancy admitted to herself pensively. Why, if she had her way, it would work out just like that... Nancy closed her eyes and let her malicious thoughts drift through her evil mind.

Maria struggled up the basement stairs with the heavy bag of flour in her arms. A puff of white powder billowed up as she dropped it down on the counter, and she paused to wipe her brow with a corner of her apron.

Suddenly, a sob escaped her lips as she crossed herself again and again, praying for help and guidance from the Lord. "Oh dear God, what is happening to my sweet Jessie?" she cried. She could only hope that now that a ransom note had been delivered, her baby would be back home very soon.

I will not forgive them if anything happens to her, she thought with conviction. As it is, they will rot in Hell for what they have done.

She saw her husband, Martin, crossing the yard from the kitchen window and raised her eyes to the ceiling. "Please, Dios Mio,

help us all do what is right to get our baby back safely." Looking out
at Martin once again, she added, "Heaven help us all."

As Brad walked away from the house, he looked back up at the
window of Nancy's bedroom where he had just left her, totally satiated.
He smiled and whistled a happy tune as he went over to retrieve his
racket and bag before calling it a day.

What a woman, he thought with admiration. She's an old
broad, but not bad in the sack. He shook his head as he remembered
some of the unbelievable things she had let him do to her. He had
never known a woman who liked sex as much as Nancy did. And he
planned to stick around and get all that he could out of this gig, he
decided.

He thought about her husband, that wimp Bill, and gave a snort
of disgust. What kinda guy would let his wife do whatever she wanted
– with whoever she wanted -- right in his own house? Not him, he
said proudly to himself. He'd kill a guy if he messed with his wife,
that's for sure.

Then there was the brat, Jessica. Good riddance, he thought
with satisfaction. He knew about the ransom note, and conjured up a
picture of all that cold cash in one big pile. Oh, what he could do with
that.

Yeah, Nancy was good for him right now. In fact, he thought to himself as he walked to his car, I'd do just about anything for her, *whatever she wants...*

Martin closed the tool shed and fastened the latch securely. He headed back towards his cottage, his mind heavy with concern about Jessica. It was all he thought about lately. His wife had told him about the ransom note that morning, with tears coursing down her cheeks. What was going to happen to them, he wondered?

As he unlocked his front door, he took off his muddy shoes and left them outside. He padded across the small front room to the little kitchen and sat down heavily at the table. After a few minutes, he looked up and saw the candles his Maria had placed amongst some flowers with a picture of Jessica in the middle. He murmured a prayer and crossed himself as he lowered his head, "Please guide me and help me, Lord, for I do not know what to do."

He remained in deep prayer for some time, as the silent tears ran down his rugged, weary face.

Bill put down the thick file he had been trying to study, rubbing his tired eyes. He wasn't sleeping hardly at all anymore. Until his little girl was found safely, he would never stop worrying. He thought about the ransom note and what the police had said when they talked to him about it. They had offered little hope of finding Jessica before the forty-eight hours was up, and told him to go ahead and try to get the money together. Bill didn't even care about the money -- he'd give the kidnappers everything he had in return for having Jessica back safely.

As he had done every minute of every day for a month now, Bill wondered where she was and what she was doing, and of course if she was safe or lying hurt somewhere. His stomach turned and he clutched himself as the pain ripped through him. He couldn't take much more, or his mind would snap. Already, he had felt on the verge of violent abandon several times in the past few days. If he could find the people who did this to his daughter, he wasn't sure now if he could stop himself from committing yet another crime and killing them with his bare hands.

Chapter Fifteen

Luke re-read the short file before him, noting with some small satisfaction that Brad had one previous arrest on his record. Two years before, Brad had been involved in a scheme to embezzle funds from a local health club. Unfortunately, he had gotten off with probation when his lawyer had proved reasonable doubt of his direct participation in the plan carried out by a group of several other people.

Other than that one time, Brad was clean as a whistle. Damn. He sure wasn't getting anywhere fast with this case. The computer had shown the name of Luis Fernandez to be so prevalent in the state of California alone that it was impossible to make any definite connection to the case. The paper used in the note had been traced to a stationery store where hundreds of reams of the stuff was sold every month, and so a dead end on that count. The model and type of the obviously ancient typewriter used had been determined, but it would be nearly impossible to trace it back to a particular person or location.

So where did that leave them? His partners were re-evaluating and re-interviewing the individuals out at the house, but so far nothing new had come up. Luke racked his brain for where to look next.

His thoughts drifted to Danni, and he smiled as he remembered the determined look on her face when she had marched into the office and demanded to see the ransom note. He had sent her back home after her little excursion to the department and she said she'd wait for him to call with further development. He now knew for sure that he had his hands full with his pretty little wife, and he had better get used to it.

He began to think about the psychic impressions and visions she had written about in her notebook. Suddenly, his mind clicked: Castello de San Carlos or San Carmello, a dark skinned, dark haired man, a ransom note written by someone with poor English, her vision of a poor, secluded village near an ocean, the name Luis Fernandez. It all seemed to add up to one thing to him -- Mexico.

Wondering if he could possibly be even close in his guessing game, he thought of one avenue he hadn't considered yet: the phone company. Quickly, he flipped through his rolodex file and found the card he was looking for: that of a contact he had in the utility's office that had helped him several times in the past. He dialed the number and was relieved to hear the woman's voice on the other end of the line, saying she would be glad to help. Now he would just have to wait a little while until she called me back to let him know she had the records he was looking for. He drummed his fingers impatiently on his desk as he starred at the phone, deep in thought.

At that same moment, Danni was starring at her phone at home. She had just had a most disturbing call and was still trying to digest what it could mean.

The caller had obviously been a male, with a deep, raspy voice or else someone disguising his voice to sound that way. After she answered, the person had said simply, *"Keep away if you know what's good for you."* and then promptly hung up.

"Keep away? From what?" she wondered as she replaced the receiver slowly. Could he have possibly meant keep away from her search for Jessica? It seemed unreal, and she doubted that was it, but what else could it be? She certainly wasn't close to finding out who was responsible for Jessica's disappearance as far as she knew, so who would want to threaten her about it? For once, her psychic ability was apparently turned off, since she didn't pick up a single clue.

She puzzled over the evasive answer for a few more minutes before deciding she had better call Luke on this one. He would have a fit if she didn't.

Luke jumped as his phone rang, and he immediately was amazed at the possibility that his phone company contact already had the information he had requested. When he heard Danni's voice, he leaned back and smiled.

"Hi, princess. Sorry I haven't called, but there's no news yet." He assumed that was the reason for her call.

"I'm sorry to hear that, honey. But actually I wanted to tell you about a strange call I just received myself."

Luke sat up straight in his chair, the fear creating a lump in his throat. "What happened, Danni? Tell me *exactly* what happened."

She did, and he made her repeat the words she had heard three times before he was convinced she wasn't leaving anything out. "I don't like the sound of this, Danni. I want you to make sure all the doors are locked and keep the dogs with you at all times. We may have a really *sick* person on our hands, and I don't want you to take any chances. I'll be home as soon as I can."

She smiled at his concern, but assured him, "Don't be ridiculous, Luke. I'm perfectly fine here. No one knows where we live, and even if they did, there's no reason to think someone would want to harm me, for heaven's sake."

"Don't be so sure of that," he demanded. "Now do as I say, and don't leave the house. I'm going to tell the Captain about this and maybe he'll let me at least arrange for a patrol to come by the house, just in case."

She still thought he was going overboard, as usual, in his over protectiveness, but she had already learned not to argue with him. "Okay, I promise. But please don't worry about hurrying home to me, I'd rather that you stay there and concentrate on finding Jessica."

They spoke for several more minutes before hanging up, Luke still deeply troubled by this turn of events, and Danni innocently void of any worry on her own behalf. She spent the remainder of the day cleaning house, and later talked for a half hour on the phone with Peggy, whom she deliberately did not tell about her mysterious caller earlier.

Chapter Sixteen

As soon as Luke got the call he had been waiting for from the phone company, he requested that the records be faxed to him and then raced over to the machine to wait for the transmission. Eight pages of phone calls from the Piedmont household came through before the machine beeped, signaling completion of the transfer.

He took the pages over to his desk where he smoothed them out and began to study them, highlighting the numbers he was looking for. Bingo. Unless there was some other explanation, someone at that house was making an awful lot of International calls to an out-of-the-way town in Mexico.

Luke frowned as he wondered about the difficulty of getting the Mexican police to cooperate with this investigation without more evidence than he had in front of him. Also, there was the possibility that the FBI should be brought in if it became an International incident. But then he was *sure* they wouldn't consider his "hunches" as enough proof to go on.

In any event, he knew he had to keep digging on his own -- the clock was ticking, and every minute that went by brought them closer to the time when the kidnappers would make their final demands. As past experience had proven, one of the most dangerous times for a kidnap victim was during the ransom exchange process. Luke began to make his calls.

Danni sat curled up on the couch by the fireplace, her feet tucked beneath her. The dogs were sleeping lazily nearby, her cats elsewhere in the house. She had followed Luke's orders, grudgingly, and checked the doors to make sure they were all locked before settling down to think.

She went over the impressions she had gleaned from speaking with the various people at the house, then decided to put them aside since she had come up with nothing really conclusive and neither had Luke. Stymied, she got up to go make a cup of coffee, and reached into the drawer to get a spoon. The memory of the scorpions came speeding back to her and she peeked in to make sure she saw none this time. Laughing at her silliness, she took her mug back to the couch and resettled herself on the comfortable cushions.

She began to consider the scorpion episode once again, and then thought about the snake in the mailbox. She had never mentioned either to Luke. And what about the menacing phone call? If she put them all together, that made three occasions that could actually be considered "threatening" acts against her within a short span of time. And all since she became involved with Jessica's disappearance. Was it possible? Or was she just grasping at straws? She admitted ruefully that it was an awfully big coincidence, if that was the case.

Then, her mind floated back over the various "glimpses" she had experienced over the past month. She picked up a piece of scratch paper and a pencil and made a simple list:

1.   inside dark room, scared, distinct smell of chili

2.   ocean, hills, wind on face, tall grass

3.   in doorway of library, arguing couple, cold, *intense hate*

4.   same ocean, hills, tall grass, village, sign (Castello de San Carlos / Carmello)

5.   ransom note: coffee stain, man with dark skin/hair/scar on cheek, terrible smell

6.   name: Luis Fernandez

Danni sat and stared at the list, her pencil tapping pensively on her thigh. She closed her eyes then, and tried to join all of the sensations from her list into one picture ...one *feeling*...one *place.* If she willed herself hard enough, perhaps she could make herself find the place: where...where...where was it...

Suddenly she had it. With the exception of the vision about the fighting couple at Jessica's home, the rest of her glimpses had clearly one thing in common: Mexico. It had to be. Danni reasoned that there were certainly many Spanish towns in California and New Mexico, but none as small and poor as the village she had seen in her mind -- and none so close to the ocean either.

As a feeling of excitement overcame her, she put down her paper and her mug and raced to find an almanac. She flipped open the book to find the map of Mexico and then let her fingers race across the page. Where in Mexico was the question. She immediately eliminated the gulf coastline, knowing instinctively the place she was looking for was on the Baja side. It was becoming clearer now. She was sure she was closing in on the location now. Finally, she picked up her pencil and circled a small area of coastline about 150 to 250 miles south of the U. S. border. There was no town listed by the name of San Carlos or San Carmello, but she knew she was right. She just *knew it.*

There was now no question in her mind as to her next action. She would go down there herself and find Jessica. Thoughts of possible danger didn't even enter her mind as she raced into her bedroom and began packing a small suitcase haphazardly.

One of her cats jumped up on the bed and meowed at her, and she reached out to stroke it's fur absentmindedly. Oh -- the pets. She ran out to pick up the phone and dial Peggy. She wasn't sure when or if Luke would be home to feed them, and that was one thing she wouldn't take a chance on. Peggy was busy with a customer at that moment, but Danni insisted on holding until she was available. She was just too excited to wait for a return call.

"Hi there. What's up?" Peggy asked brightly.

"I need you to take care of my pets for a couple of days. I'm not sure how many. I'm, ah, going out of town for a while." Danni knew she sounded mysterious and cursed herself for not thinking of a better excuse before calling Peggy.

Sure enough, Peggy was not about to settle for Danni's vague reason for needing a pet-sitter. "Hold on, now. Exactly where are you going? And I assume Luke is going with you? When did you decide on this trip? I just talked to you a while ago and you didn't mention anything then."

Danni smiled as she listened to her friend ramble on with all her questions, not giving Danni a chance to get a word in edgewise. Finally, when Peggy ran out of breath, she jumped in, deciding to be truthful with her. There was just no time to be inventive at this point.

"I'm going down to Mexico. I think that's where Jessica is being held, and I've got what you could call a 'hot' feeling right now. I think I can find her if I go right away."

"WHAT? ARE YOU CRAZY?" Peggy yelled without concern about her boss and the three lady patrons that were staring at her incredulously in the dress shop.

"Now calm down, Peggy. I'll be fine. I'm just going to go find out where she is, and then I'll call for help. I'm not stupid enough to try to rescue her all by myself, you know."

But Peggy still wasn't going for it. "Does Luke know about this?" she asked pointedly.

"Well, not exactly," Danni admitted. "He would only try to stop me from going and I just can't let that happen, not at this point. You have to understand. I don't know how long I'll have this 'feeling'. It may fade away if I wait too long."

Peggy was shaking her head in confusion now, not sure if she could comprehend what her friend was experiencing, and certainly not sure if she should continue trying to stop her from going on this wild goose chase. "I don't know, Danni, what if..."

But Danni interrupted her, becoming frustrated as she realized the minutes were flying by while she was trying to convince Peggy to help her out. "Never mind 'what if', Peg. Now just say you'll come over after work. You have a key, and you know where all the food and stuff is. Just walk the dogs in the evening and let the cats out for a while. That's all you have to do. Okay?"

Peggy hesitated, and then thought of little Jessica trapped in her terrifying situation and relented. "Okay. But promise me you won't do anything foolish. We don't need to lose you now, too."

Danni smiled and reassured her, "Don't worry. I promise. And thanks, pal. I owe you one."

Danni hung up and went to pack to her suitcase. She was just trying to find her heavy boots to wear when she heard the front door slam shut. Luke was home. Damn.

Chapter Seventeen

Danni didn't have time to think of hiding the suitcase or even moving from the spot where she had been standing when Luke burst into the bedroom and took in everything in one swift glance.

"Would you mind explaining what you're doing? I don't think I've done anything that would warrant your moving out on me quite yet, so what's with the suitcase?"

Danni looked guiltily down at her clothes stuffed into the piece of luggage and then turned away from his direct gaze before answering. "I'm just going on a little trip, that's all."

"And I don't suppose you'd like to tell me -- your *husband* -- *where* you are thinking of going? Not to mention answering the question of whether or not you were going to tell me about your plans *before* you left, or just let me sit and casually wonder where my wife had *disappeared to*." His voice had risen dramatically as he spoke, and Danni shrunk back from his challenging words. The thought crossed her mind briefly that he certainly did have the Italian temper to go with his heritage.

"I didn't have time. I.." she began weakly.

Suddenly, Luke walked over to her and pulled her into his arms, closing his eyes and taking a deep breath before he spoke softly into her ear. "I'm sorry I yelled at you, bella. I just don't know what I'd do if I ever lost you. I've only just recently *found* you. I *need* you, my love. You're my life now, like the blood that flows in my veins, the air that I breathe. Don't you understand that?"

Danni leaned away slightly and gazed into his loving eyes, filled with truth and concern about her. She sighed as she realized she must tell him everything, and hope he would understand her need to leave, and soon.

She held his hand and guided him back into the living room where they sat down on the couch together. She retrieved her slip of paper from the floor. Danni calmly and quickly summarized her thoughts and feelings from re-examining her visions and how it had led her to the conclusion that Jessica was being held in Mexico. She pulled out the map and showed him the area she had circled earlier.

Luke was strangely quiet for a few minutes, and Danni wondered what his reaction was going to be. Was he going to tell her she was crazy to go all the way to Mexico on nothing but a 'feeling'? Would he laugh at her naivety? Or worse, would he just dismiss her conclusion as ridiculous and insist she forget the whole thing?

When Luke finally spoke, he was deadly serious. "Danni, I came home early to tell you about some ideas I have of my own about Jessica's whereabouts." Danni was curious to hear what he had to say, but was still anxious to be on her way and wished he would hurry up and say whatever he had to say.

Danni waited silently, and Luke went on. "You see, I sort of came to the same conclusion as you did about the possibility of Mexico being the location where Jessica is being held. And to add to my feelings, I got a list of the Piedmont's phone calls over the last month and there were numerous ones to a big city -- you guessed it -- in Mexico.

He saw Danni's eyes light up with excitement, but he held up his hand to stop her from interrupting, and then went on. "Just to be sure, I called Bill at his office and asked if he had made any of the calls, or whether he thought perhaps Maria or Martin could have used the phone in his absence. Bill said that he certainly had not made the calls, and he was sure they had not either since all of their relatives live here in Santa Bella, as far as he knows. Bill said he would be going home soon and would ask them personally, but he felt positive this was a clue to the kidnapping." Until we can prove she's in Mexico, though, we don't have any official jurisdiction down there – even the FBI would just laugh at us.

"Really? So you agree, then. We should go to Mexico right away." she stood up and grabbed his hand, pulling him towards the bedroom to pack.

"Wait a minute, sweetheart," he grabbed her arm and turned her back towards him. "Who said anything about 'us' going? I certainly

134

don't need you along with me. You'll only give me one more thing to worry about."

Danni narrowed her eyes and crossed her arms, a familiarly defiant look settling upon her face. "That's where you're wrong, Detective Reghetti. On several counts. First, the phone calls you found were made to a big city, and that is obviously *not* the tiny place where she is being held. I'm the only one who can find the village, *remember*? When I see the place, I'll know it. You could wander around the countryside for weeks and never know which town it was." She ticked off her fingers, as she counted her reasons for going.

"Secondly, I would probably be in more danger staying here than if I were with you, my darling husband. Don't forget about that threatening phone call. And by the way, I've decided that the snake in the mailbox and the scorpions in the drawer were also a part of someone's attempt to scare me off. And thirdly, I would only follow after you by myself anyway, and in that case I'd probably be in much more danger than ever."

"Scorpions? Snakes? What's all this about?" Luke asked incredulously.

"Never mind. I'll tell you all about it on the way. Let's just get going. Every minute counts."

Luke realized that he actually would feel safer having Danni by his side. At least that way he could watch over her and not be constantly worried about her safety while he was gone. And he admitted, finally, that she really was the only one would could positively identify the village in her vision with absolute certainty.

"Well, okay. But you'll do exactly as I say -- with no arguments, right?"

"Right." Danni smiled at him and winked. Somehow Luke was sure she was merely saying what he wanted to hear, but there was no time to worry about it now. He'd just have to keep her in line, that was all.

Chapter Eighteen

Luke and Danni were just about ready to hop in the car and race to the airport for a flight to San Diego when the phone rang. Worried that it might be Peggy reneging on her promise to take care of her beloved pets and too excited to use her innate capabilities, Danni insisted on answering it. But it wasn't Peggy; it was Bill. He asked to speak to Luke.

Danni stood by quietly listening to a non-informative one-sided conversation until Luke hung up with a strange look on his face. "What's the matter?" she asked.

"Bill said he just got home and it's the strangest thing..." he hesitated as he tried to figure it out in his mind.

"*What is*?" Danni asked impatiently. Her psychic awareness was obviously in an "off" mode at the moment.

"Well, it seems that the house is deserted. Everyone is gone. Nancy, Maria, Martin. Brad left a note that he wouldn't be over for a few days. And Jim left a message on the answering machine saying he was going out of town on a job and would call when he got back."

"Maybe Nancy and Brad left together?" Danni suggested. "In a way, I wish they would, so poor Bill could get on with a divorce and be done with her."

"And Jim? And Maria and Martin? It's just too big of a coincidence, Danni. I think I should call the Captain and let him know about this."

Danni couldn't argue with his decision and knew the few minutes it took to call were a necessary delay. Danni waited patiently as Luke reached his boss and began talking. She noticed, however, that Luke did not mention the fact that they were on their way to Mexico, and she asked him about it when he hung up.

He shrugged his shoulders and responded, "I know my boss, honey. He would insist we go through the normal 'channels' before going down there. And like you, I just don't think we have the time to do that right now. We'll call him from across the border, that way he won't be able to do much but wish us luck," he smiled grimly.

"Good idea. Now you're thinking more like me." Danni said with a determined smile.

Luke groaned out loud at the thought, and they proceeded to put their two small suitcases into the car, making sure all the pets were secured in the house before leaving for the airport.

Chapter Nineteen

They were strangely silent during their drive to the Santa Bella airport on the outskirts of town near the University. Both Luke and Danni were engrossed in their own thoughts and concerns about the next day or so. Each was unaware of the other's concurrence that their actions might be the worst possible avenue they could take, but neither was willing *not* to take the chance.

Danni's feelings were stronger than ever now. Since she had come to the conclusion she must go to Mexico, it was almost as if an invisible giant magnet was pulling her faster and faster towards her intended goal. She couldn't help but feel a little intimidated by these new sensations sweeping over her, practically taking over her will to do as she pleased. Perhaps it was because she had never used her abilities in such a way before that affected others so profoundly -- the very life or death of a person, in fact -- that she was experiencing this degree of newfound strength of conviction. She didn't really know, and at this point did not want to take the time to think about it -- or anything for that matter -- other than Jessica.

Luke was going through his own myriad emotions, like a roller coaster with its ups and downs. One minute he was sure they were doing the right thing, and that he needed Danni by his side to help him and at the same time keep her safe. The next minute he was tempted to turn the car around and drive straight back home, certain that they were being foolhardy and deliberately putting themselves in a dangerous situation. Then, in his final analysis, he came to the realization that it was too late to turn back now. He could see it as he glanced sideways at Danni. They would go to Mexico together regardless of the jeopardy to their own lives and try to save that of a young girl who had touched their hearts and souls.

As he settled on that last thought, he reached over and took Danni's hand, squeezing it with love. Maybe when this was all over with, they could get busy on producing a child of their own. They hadn't discussed it, but somehow he knew that this was something they both wanted as soon as possible.

Brad gulped the last swallow of his scotch and soda, and signaled the bartender for another drink. He had to think carefully before he went ahead with his plan. After all, you only got one chance like this in a lifetime, and this was his.

With a grim smile, He thought back to when he had overheard Bill talking to Nancy about the ransom note that had been delivered to them. Bill was saying how he was going to make some phone calls and start getting the money together, and Nancy was, as usual, arguing about whether or not he should do it. Of course the old man wanted to hand over the cash, but ol' Nance, well, she was as tight-fisted as you could get and wanted the police department to somehow put some fake money up for the ransom. Of course, Bill had won out, telling her he didn't care what she thought, that it was obvious she had never cared about Jessica's well-being from the start and certainly didn't now.

But the point was that Bill could just up and make a few calls and arrange for all that dough -- just that easy. Anyone who could do that, Brad reasoned, didn't really need all that money in the first place. Man, what he could do with that kinda money, he thought to himself slightly drunkenly. Yeah, it would serve them all right. He would do it. That's why he had left the note about his being gone for a few days, that way he'd have time to work out the rest of the details.

Luke and Danni's flight down to San Diego was uneventful, and they quickly secured a rental vehicle for their use in driving across the border. They deliberately picked an all-terrain type jeep with four-wheel drive, since they didn't know what kind of situations they might shortly find themselves in. As Danni completed the final forms for Mexican insurance, Luke touched her arm and said, "I think I should go call the Captain again now...I'm anxious to see if anyone from the house has turned up since we last talked to him."

Danni nodded her approval and Luke proceeded to find the nearest telephone. But Luke came walking back towards Danni just minutes later, looking slightly confused and annoyed. "He wasn't there, damn it. In fact, all the guys on the case are out on the street right now, and the dispatcher couldn't tell me anything new. He said the Captain was expected back at any minute and told me to call back."

Danni picked up her bag, holding the jeep keys in her other hand. "There isn't time, Luke. We just can't sit around this airport waiting to catch your boss in, while the kidnappers may be getting ready to move Jessica any minute."

Luke sighed, and then agreed with her. "I guess you're right. We can always call from down in Mexico. We might have more information for him by then anyway."

So it was decided unanimously, and together they found their transportation and jumped in, heading for the border.

Maria was still not familiar with the steering on her boss' big car she had borrowed. She had decided to follow her husband when she had seen him acting very strange soon after they had talked about the ransom note. She had secretly watched him go to their cottage and pack a single small bag. Realizing he was going somewhere without her, Maria made up her mind quickly to take her boss' old station wagon and see where her husband was going.

She had been sincerely worried about him lately. For weeks he had become more and more distant to her, so different than the loving, wonderful Martin she had been married to for over twenty years. The only answer in her mind was that somehow Martin was going to try and find Jessica and did not want to take her, Maria, in case there was trouble. Well, Maria did not care what kind of trouble there might be -- she was going to be there to help her husband no matter what he thought.

The problem on her mind right now, though, was in gaining complete control of this huge station wagon. She had not driven any other car besides their own small Toyota for many years, and it was difficult handling this strange, ungainly automobile. She also began to wonder how far they were driving as Martin neared the Santa Bella city limits going south on Highway 101. She was glad she had money for gas in her purse -- she was determined to follow Martin as long as it took to see where he was headed.

Jim was on the road at the same time as the others, only going in another direction. Once he had made up his mind to go through with his decision, he had not looked back or thought of the consequences.

As he drove, he chain smoked and played loud music on the car radio, trying to block out the subconscious thoughts that were threatening to change his mind. No, he told himself firmly, this time he was really going to finish what he started, not like all the other times in the past.

Finally, a clear image of the girl in the photograph on his wall appeared in his mind and he focused on that while he drove, oblivious to everyone and everything else around him.

Chapter Twenty

The Captain had just returned from the field and was headed towards his office when the detective approached him. "Sir, Mr. Piedmont is on the line for you -- he's just received a call from the kidnappers with instructions on where to drop off the ransom money."

The determination was evident on the Captain's face as he walked rapidly into his office and grabbed the telephone line that was blinking. He listened carefully while Mr. Piedmont repeated word for word the instructions that the kidnappers had given him. Mr. Piedmont was to deliver the money in unmarked bills inside of a briefcase to a particular private beach access road at sunrise tomorrow morning. The caller had stressed that there was only one road in and that if anyone else besides Mr. Piedmont himself were seen in the vicinity, the girl would be killed instantly.

Mr. Piedmont had been frantic with worry that the police would insist on accompanying him to the drop-off site, and he was adamant that he didn't care about the money, only in getting his daughter back alive. The Captain realized he would not be able to reason with Mr. Piedmont in his current state, and told him to wait before doing anything rash; he would be right over to talk with him personally.

After hanging up the line, the Captain frowned. He was perplexed by the kidnapper's call. First, it was usual for the method of contact to be the same. In other words, he had expected another note, not a call. Second, they were to have been given until tomorrow *night at midnight* to raise the money. This call seemed to be jumping the gun. But he knew from experience that you couldn't discount anything when you were dealing with fanatics. He would do what he could to check out the validity of the call – check the wiretaps he had installed --before talking with Mr. Piedmont and advising him what to do.

It was early evening by the time Luke and Danni arrived in the town of Rosario, Mexico. This was the place where the series of telephone calls had been made to from the Piedmont household. As the remaining light of day was fading fast, Luke convinced Danni that they would have to spend the night there, and resume their search the next morning.

They found a small but clean little inn where they checked in and went straight to their room. They sat next to each other on the tiny bed, the only piece of furniture in the room besides a small, worn dresser.

Frustrated with the time they would be wasting, Danni said plaintively, "At least we can go out and ask some questions of a few people, can't we? I hate not being able to do anything but wait. We've come so far."

Her protest was overruled by Luke who answered, "Oh yeah. I can just see us going up to somebody and saying 'Hey, do you know where the bad guys are keeping the kidnapped kid?' That would go over real well, especially if we're at all close with our suspicion that she really might be in this area."

After hitting Luke on the arm for his sarcastic remark, Danni countered, "I *know* Jessica's near here somewhere, don't ask me how, but I'm sure of it. Anyway, we need to get something to eat, so we have to go out." She stuck her tongue out at him and made a face.

Shaking his head and smiling, Luke relented. "Okay, we'll go find a place to eat. But *no questions*, promise?"

Getting that same look of devilment that Luke was beginning to become quite familiar with, Danni responded sweetly, "Of course, sweetheart. Whatever you say. _You are_ the *boss* of the family, after all."

It was easy to follow their noses to a quaint little outdoor cantina near where they were staying and they enjoyed the short walk as they observed the local color. Even at this hour, children ran everywhere, giggling and babbling away to each other and passing adults including Luke, who spoke only a few words of Spanish, and Danni who spoke absolutely none. She thought ruefully of her several years of Italian she had taken, and although some of the words were quite alike, she could not make out what they were saying at all.

147

Luke ordered their meals and some ice cold cervezas to wash it down with. While they ate, they began to plan their actions for the next day, as Danni's eyes continuously roved around the room.

"You wouldn't possibly be thinking of talking to any of these people, now, would you princess?" Luke asked skeptically.

"Who, me?" Danni replied innocently. "I wouldn't think of such a thing. What a strange question to ask, my darling dearest sweetheart."

"Oh boy, now I know I'm in trouble. Look, just don't call attention to us any more than we already have by being here in the first place. We'll never find out anything useful that way, and it may make things worse, for Heaven's sake."

Danni looked hurt as she said, "You don't have to tell me that. I know. I know." Then, noticing that people were indeed beginning to look and nod in their direction, Danni lowered her voice and went on. "I'm sorry. I'll behave. Now tell me again what we're going to do in the morning."

Luke wiped his mouth with his napkin, and then said in a low voice, "We'll leave at sunrise and take some fruit, bread and soft drinks with us so we won't have to stop at all for food. We'll head towards the coast and you'll see if you can pick up any familiar scenes from your memory. We've already covered some of the area you circled on the map on the way down here. You said it had to be on or near the ocean, right?"

"Yes, I think we're heading in the right direction. I feel like we're really close. I guess it's no use asking if we could leave any earlier?"

Luke shook his head, saying "No, we need our rest and we wouldn't be able to see anything clearly in the moonlight anyway. We'll wait until sunrise, then start right out."

After finishing their delicious food, they walked back towards their inn. Danni suddenly felt the strangest sensation that they were being watched and shivered uncontrollably. "Are you okay, honey?" Luke asked with concern.

"Yes, I just, oh, it's nothing. I'm just worn out after all this activity in one day, that's all."

Luke agreed, hugging her tight as they walked. "Just as I said, you need your rest, probably even more than I do. I would imagine that using all that 'mental' energy is more exhausting than a physical workout," he said with concern in his voice.

Danni nodded and smiled, but still had the nagging feeling that unfriendly eyes were upon them. Luke stopped at the desk at the inn and asked if he could use a telephone to make a long distance call to the States. The kind, older man who was the manager said there was no public phone, but if Luke was willing to pay -- in United States dollars -- they could use the phone in his room for the call. Luke and Danni readily agreed to this arrangement, and they were led into a room not much bigger than their own, but with a small black and white television and a phone on a table by the door.

It took only a few minutes longer than usual for the call to go through and Luke heard the line ringing at his department's office. He asked to be put through to the Captain, and was told he should hold, that the Captain was on another line but wanted to speak to him -- *badly.* Luke gulped as he whispered to Danni what he had been told, and she patted him on the back reassuringly.

When the Captain came on the phone, Luke's fears were not eased. "Reghetti. Where are you? Exactly?"

"Well, sir, we're in a town called Rosario about 200 miles south of the border. You see, sir, my wife -- you remember, she's psychic -- and well, she had this feeling..."

"I'm really not interested in her *feelings* right now, Reghetti. What I *am* interested in is getting you back here in front of me so I can personally wring your neck for running off on a damn wild goose chase when we're in the middle of meeting ransom demands at this very minute."

"What? I..." Luke stammered, realizing that the Captain's voice was rising uncontrollably and unsure of what he was being told.

"That's right. Piedmont got a call just a few minutes ago from the perps laying out the rules for the drop-off. And where is my star detective? On a honeymoon in Mexico. Well, fine. Never mind rushing back up here, kid. We'll handle everything at this end. You and your psychic wife can just take an *extended vacation* down there for all I care. In fact, don't bother to hurry coming back."

The line went dead in Luke's ear and he carefully laid the phone down as he looked up into Danni's bewildered face. He explained briefly about the call from the kidnappers but left out the Captain's violent reaction to Luke's insubordination. He would worry about that later. Right now, he had to think -- what did this latest development mean?

As if reading his mind, Danni said firmly, "I don't care if they got a hundred calls, Luke. We're on the right track, honey, I know we are."

Luke smiled weakly as he brought her into his arms. "I hope so. Anyway, I guess it won't hurt to satisfy our curiosity down here. I've, ah, been given a little time off, it seems."

Danni kissed him tenderly and replied, "It doesn't matter. Nothing does except finding Jessica. And you'll see, we're almost there."

With that, they walked slowly up to their room and lay down to sleep in each other's arms, not aware of the man who had watched them from the street just outside the door of the inn.

Chapter Twenty-One

The Captain was just about to leave the office and go up to meet with Mr. Piedmont at his house to discuss the kidnappers' call when his secretary interrupted him. She handed him an envelope and said it had just been delivered with instructions to be given to him directly, and no one else.

He thanked her and she went back to her desk, while he studied the plain envelope with his name on it in big bold letters. He slipped on a pair of plastic gloves before he handled it even more, and then gingerly opened it and pulled out the single sheet of paper within.

As he unfolded it, his eyes scanned the few sentences and the pieces began to fall into place in his mind. This was the true ransom note, he now knew; and the call had been a fake all along just as he had suspected. Putting aside what he would do with the fake caller's demands, he concentrated on the note before him:

WE NO YOU ARE IN CHARG SO WE GIVE THIS TO YOU. DO THIS OR THE GIRL WILL BE KILT. SHE WILL NOT BE FOUND, FOR SURE. THE FATHER IS TO TAKE THE MONEY IN HIS PLANE. HE MUST BE A-LON. WE NO HE

CAN FLY THE PLANES. THE FLIT PLANS IS IN THE PLANE. HE MUST LEAF AT NOON TOMORRO. WE WILL GIVE HIM MORE INFORMASION ON THE PLANE RADIO. DO NOT TRY TO TRIC US. WE WILL NO. THE GIRL WILL DYE AND HER DEATH WILL BE ON YOUR HEADS FOREVER.

The Captain immediately called in his staff and began making appropriate arrangements to handle the 'fake' kidnap call. He also sent a detective out to the airport to find the plane and retrieve the flight plan. At least then they would know where Piedmont was expected to fly tomorrow. He decided not to say anything just yet to Piedmont. He would be really agitated when he learned of this latest development, and the Captain needed a little time to work things out in his mind before that happened. "Damn that Reghetti. He should be here helping us on this," he thought crossly.

He had just hung up from dispatching the last person handling the fake ransom demands when his line began blinking once again. It was his man at the airport calling in the flight plan destination: the coastal area along Baja just south of the US border. The note had said Piedmont would get further instructions via radio once he got into their airspace -- *Mexican* airspace.

"Damn and double damn," he muttered as he slammed his fist down on his desk so violently that several reports and folders slid off the edge to the floor. "That's right where Reghetti and his wife are. How in hell did they know..."

He stopped suddenly and stormed out of his office towards Luke's cubicle. It only took him a few minutes of rummaging to locate the copies of the phone call ledgers from the Piedmont house, with circles around the numbers Luke had found to be of interest. "I'll really kill him now," he said as he grabbed the pages and strode back into his office, thinking, "...if the perps don't kill him first."

The Captain began barking orders right and left: Try to find Reghetti. Get the Mexican consulate on the phone. Call our contact at the FBI. In the middle of all this, his secretary walked in with the information he had asked her for soon after receiving the note: who had delivered it? Had they been seen and was an ID made? He snorted in disgust as he heard his answer: the note had been delivered by a taxi driver who, when located, had said a dirty-faced little kid had given it to him and he wouldn't ever recognize the brat again in a million years. The Captain realized realistically that there just wasn't time to follow up on that angle anyway, so he let it go.

He made arrangements for a team of professionals to get down to Rosario as soon as possible, and could only hope that they would get there in time to be of help. Now if only Reghetti would call in just *one more time. And soon.*

Luke had been lying awake for a short time, starring into the fading darkness, when he felt Danni stir slightly beside him. He gently stroked her forehead, brushing her long silky hair away from her face and kissing her temple lovingly. "Mm.mmm.mm..." she murmured sleepily. "Wha time izzit?"

"Time to rise and shine, princess. The dawn is almost upon us and we must be off to save the day." Luke said, trying to lighten his sense of impending danger for them both.

Danni struggled to sit up, rubbing her sleepy eyes, then said, "What's that over by the door?"

Luke looked down and there on the floor was a slip of paper that had obviously been pushed under the door while they slept. He started to get up to fetch it, but Danni held him back, exclaiming "No. Don't touch it. There's something...*evil*...about the person who delivered that note. OH." She gasped as she held her hand to her mouth. She had never felt such malevolence before, and didn't want to meet the person from whom it originated.

Luke calmed her down, then went to pick up the note. He read it out loud to Danni:

LEAV NOW OR YOU WILL BOTH DYE.

Luke looked up at Danni and smiled halfheartedly. "Guess we must be getting pretty close, eh?"

Danni nodded and tried to control her shaking body. "Oh, Luke! I can't stand the thought of a person like that having poor little Jessica. Come on, hurry! Let's get going."

Proud of his wife for her determination and concern for others over her own safety, he quickly followed her lead and they were ready to leave in a few short minutes. Luke checked his gun, and tucked it into the front of his pants within easy reach. They tiptoed silently down the old stairs and listened at every turn for a noise or other indication that they were being watched. Luke kept Danni protected behind him as they made their way through the small lobby and out the door to their car.

"What if they've done something to the jeep?" he worried out loud.

Danni laid her palm flat on the hood for a moment, then said with certainty, "No, it's okay. After all, they did want us to leave, didn't they? Now let's go."

They were off and driving down the dirt roads towards the ocean and Danni had her head almost totally out of the window, scanning the scenery for the area they were looking for. They stopped when they were safely out of the town, and pulled over to catch their breath and calm down after their stressful wake-up scenario that morning.

Danni reached in the back seat and pulled out some fruit and bread, handing portions to Luke. They sat eating quietly, wondering how this day would turn out. At the same exact moment, they both stopped and turned to each other, gazed into the other's eyes, and then hugged one another fiercely. "I love you so much, Luke. Please be safe." Danni pleaded with heartfelt sincerity.

"I love you too, princess. And don't worry, God will help us through this."

Jim tossed the smoldering cigarette butt out his car window and strained his weary eyes to read the next road sign. He was almost there. He had driven straight through, and had only stopped for gas and coffee to keep him going. Finally, he would bring this whole thing to an end, he resolved to himself.

It was time, and soon everything would be over. Noticing his gas tank was nearing empty once again, he pulled into the next station and struggled out of the car, stretching his tired muscles after his exhausting, long drive. The sun was just rising, and he stopped for a moment to watch the colors on the horizon change from dark blues and grays to pale yellows and oranges. A new day...and a new *ending* -- finally.

He stayed close to the ground where he couldn't be seen from his hiding place behind a large boulder. His back was starting to hurt from his uncomfortable position, but he reassured himself it would all be worth it very soon.

He heard it before he saw it -- a car was driving slowly down the deserted private beach access road. It was about two hundred feet away from him now, and would have to slow to a stop soon in front of the padlocked gate that barred the way. His gaze once again scanned the hillside, then the beach in both directions for signs of others, but he saw nothing. He began to feel slightly elated, and if he had not stopped himself in time, he would have giggled out loud.

This was easier than he thought it would be. Soon he'd be on his way -- free of the necessity to work ever again. His hand reached over to grab for the bullhorn he was intending to use for his final instructions to Mr. Piedmont, when he felt a piece of cold, heavy metal pressed up against his forehead. Somehow his feeling of elation disappeared instantaneously and instead Brad began suffering a case of extreme nausea.

Maria decided she could not stand this craziness any longer. The next time Martin stopped for gas she was going to pull up behind him, then confront him and find out what in the world he was doing. Her chance came just ten minutes later when he pulled into a gas station on the outskirts of the small town of Rosario. Maria sped up and pulled up next to him, watching his face turn to a look of horror as he saw her step out of the station wagon and walk towards him.

Chapter Twenty-Two

After finishing their quick snack, Luke and Danni drove on down the coast. Suddenly, Danni screamed, "Stop!" She pointed to an area just in front of them. "There. I think that's it."

Luke swerved the jeep to the edge of the road, then stopped and looked around. The ocean crashed against the jagged rocks at the bottom of the cliff where they were parked. Tall grass grew wild in every direction, swaying slightly in the breeze. Danni felt the sea mist on her face and reached up to touch her cheek as she stepped out and looked around. Luke joined her, watching her silently as she took in everything as if in a dream.

"I feel it, Luke. This is the place where I was in my vision. I'm sure of it."

Luke reached for her hand and pulled her away from the threatening cliff nearby. "Where do we go now, Danni?" he asked gently.

She pointed towards a hill in the distance and they decided to walk as the ground was quite muddy in places and they were afraid the jeep would get stuck. Also, Danni assured him it wasn't far, and they wanted to arrive unbeknownst to anyone else, if at all possible.

The sun was rising rapidly by the time they reached the top of the hill and stood looking down at the village that lay below, exactly as Danni had predicted it would. "You're really something, kiddo," Luke said admiringly.

Danni shrugged off his compliment and replied nervously, "I just hope we're not too late."

They decided on the best avenue of approach that would hopefully keep them the most protected from view and walked down the hill, carefully, quietly.

Luke let Danni lead him slightly since she seemed to know exactly where to go as if she had visited this tiny village many times before. She stopped at the edge of a small outbuilding with crumbling walls and rusted windows. They both simultaneously looked up at the old wooden sign hanging crookedly directly in front of them. It read "Castello de San Carnitos" in worn, faded lettering. They glanced at each other and nodded in silent understanding that they were indeed in the right place -- the place in Danni's vision -- the place where they hoped to find Jessica before it was too late.

Luke had his gun in his hand now and the safety off. He gripped Danni's small hand in his other fist tightly. There were few people about, mostly little children who played together with a small ball that had seen better days.

Danni pointed towards a dark wooden structure at the far end of the dirt road, and they began walking, keeping as close to the buildings as possible as they tried to blend in to the background. If they had been watching the whole scene from the outside, they would have realized how much they stood out amongst the structures in the village. Their dress, not to mention their white skin, made it quite obvious they didn't belong there. But Luke and Danni could only think about poor little Jessica being held here -- by people who would probably just as soon kill her as blink their eyes.

When they finally reached the building, they saw that the windows had been boarded shut. They quickly circled around the back, but saw no easy point of entry. Finally, Luke signaled to Danni to wait behind a nearby boulder as he gripped his gun tightly, crouching low as he approached the door. Danni's breath seemed to be caught in her throat as she watched him, terrified of what might happen next.

Luke reached out and pounded on the door with the heel of his gun handle, then stepped back quickly, his back flat against the wall next to the door. Hearing no noise from within, Luke took a chance and reached out to turn the rusty, dented door handle while he remained as far from the opening as possible. Surprisingly, the door opened easily, emitting a loud creaking sound that made both Luke and Danni freeze in anticipation. But nothing happened. No one came charging out, guns blasting, as they had feared.

Luke cautiously walked into the building, swinging his gun from left to right in front of him as his eyes quickly adjusted to the darkness within.

"Where are they?" Danni asked suddenly from right behind him, startling Luke and making him jump in surprise.

"Goddamn it, Danni. I told you to stay outside." he hissed, pushing her to one side behind a lumpy old couch.

"Never mind that now, Luke. Where is Jessica?" she asked as she proceeded to walk around Luke towards the only other door in the building. The door was slightly ajar, and the dust motes floated in the musty air that surrounded them.

"Danni. Wait." Luke yelled as he ran to leap in front of her, pushing the door all the way open at the same time and again crouching in firing position, prepared for the worst.

Bill Piedmont checked the plane's dials and gauges in front of him one more time, making certain that everything was correct before he began to taxi for takeoff. He briefly thought back over the past twenty-four hours, and wondered if he would ever make it through the next few.

First the fake ransom instructions telling him to deliver the money to a deserted beach right there in Santa Bella, and now he was responding to the real ransom directions to fly to an unknown destination somewhere in Mexico. He had assured the Captain that he was capable of flying that distance; he had flown farther than that by himself before. And he certainly didn't care about the money. He had long since gathered it together and stuffed it into an old briefcase as instructed.

What he *was* worried about was whether or not the kidnappers would keep their end of the deal and deliver his daughter without harm. He was especially worried because he knew he was incapable of doing very much about it by himself, and there would be no way to let the authorities know where he was to land once he found out. The kidnappers would be monitoring all the frequencies, he was sure.

He wondered again briefly where everyone at the house had disappeared to. To be truthful, he really didn't care about his wife's whereabouts -- it would only make the divorce easier to obtain if she stayed away. But Maria and Martin -- they were truly like part of the family.

The Captain had put out missing persons bulletins on both of them, but there had been no results as yet. As far as Brad and Jim were concerned, Bill didn't have the time or energy to think about them. He needed all his strength and faculties to concentrate on getting Jessica back. Everyone else could wait. But, it was still strange...

Secure in the knowledge that his plane was prepared for takeoff, he thought to himself, "Well, this is it. Hold on, Jessie, Dad's coming." He taxied the small aircraft out onto the runway, feeling the sweat drip down his neck and back. He quickly felt for the small army knife he had tucked into his pocket; he had refused to carry any other type of weapon like the Captain had suggested. He was simply not accustomed to using a gun and would probably do more harm than good in a tense situation.

The takeoff was smooth, and soon he was gliding at about 6,000 feet out over the Pacific Ocean, close enough to the shoreline to see the tiny fishing boats and oil rigs. He glanced at his watch and saw it was exactly 12:15 p.m., and calculated the time he would arrive in Mexican airspace when he would need to begin monitoring his designated frequency for further instructions. He figured that at his current airspeed, it would take about three hours. He was satisfied that he was right on schedule -- the kidnappers' schedule, that is.

Danni saw immediately that the room was deserted, and touched Luke softly on the shoulder. "She's gone. They're all gone."

Luke slowly stood up, taking a deep breath to regain his composure and slow his wildly beating heart. "I can see that. Are you sure this is the right place?"

Danni looked around the room, and then went over to a stained and tattered mattress in one corner. She knelt down and touched it lightly with her fingers. Her face as she turned back to Luke said it all. "Yes...yes! This is definitely the place where Jessica was being held. I feel her still. She must have just recently been taken away from here.

Oh Luke. What can we do now? Where do you think they've taken her?"

Luke went to Danni and put his arms around her, holding her close. He shivered involuntarily as he looked around the dark and dreary room, with only the smelly old mattress in one corner and a hole that had been dug in the dirt floor for the young girl to relieve herself into. The outer room had only held the worn couch and a battered table with two wooden chairs. It was obvious that this had been a type of "holding cell" for Jessica and that food had been brought in for her and her captors from elsewhere.

"I don't know, princess. I just don't know." he responded without much hope to her questions.

They hugged each other in silence for a moment, and then suddenly Danni looked up into Luke's eyes and said, "Then I must try to *sense* where they have taken her."

Feeling that they had run out of time, Luke shook his head sadly, "I don't think it will help, little one. You've done so much to get us this far, but now I'm sure they're already on their way to collect their ransom. It's just too late."

"No. It's never too late," Danni said fiercely. "You said yourself we need to try and find her *before* they reach the ransom point. I have to try!"

Luke realized that he would have to relent to her pleading, even though he still believed it would be a waste of time. "Okay, tell me what you want to do and I'll try to help if I can."

Danni smiled briefly, the love and gratefulness evident in her eyes. "Thank you, my darling. Now here's what I want to do: I need to spend some time here studying every inch of this building and it's contents. Perhaps I can pick up a feeling from somewhere. It would be best if you waited outside so I can concentrate."

Luke nodded, figuring he could watch over her better from outside anyway in case anyone tried to bother them. He left her then, and Danni proceeded to walk slowly around each of the two rooms, pausing every now and then to touch a wall, or pick up an object she found. As her fingers passed over one of the chairs in the main room, she stopped -- and gasped -- as a bolt of terror ran through her.

The pockmarked face of the dark-skinned man shone with smelly perspiration as he grinned with malevolence. His teeth were yellowed and chipped, and the stubble of beard made it evident he had not shaved in many days. The first rays of the morning sun were shining through the open door of the shack as he strode towards the girl who lay pitifully curled into a ball on the mattress. "Time to go. Ahora." he sneered at her as she flinched away from his reaching hands.

Danni gulped as she felt the fear that permeated the room. She moved to the next chair and again her fingers reacted to the sensation so vividly evident there.

166

This man was not as dark, although clearly of Mexican descent. His face looked vaguely familiar, yet strangely different. She could feel his distaste for the other, meaner man and knew that he was not as bad and even felt sad about Jessica and her plight.

Then, she could see through his eyes as he pictured a place: a flat plateau high upon a mountain above the crashing ocean waves below. He had been there before -- he was very familiar with this mountaintop. He knew the way, and the other man did not. He was going to show him the way, and take the girl there. She again felt his concern for the child. He was afraid of the other man, afraid of what he might do.

Danni shook her head to cleanse her mind of the dreamlike state she had been in. She rushed outside, again surprising Luke who had been tensely waiting there for her.

"I saw where they are going, Luke. It's on top of a mountain, a flat mountain, like a plateau or something. I don't think it's too far from here, but we've got to hurry."

She started running from the village up the hill to return to their jeep and Luke had to hurry to catch up with her. As they came to the top of the small hill, they looked down upon the road and saw with relief that their jeep was still right where they had left it. Just as they were about to begin their descent, they saw several *policia* drive by at high speed.

"Do you think they're going where we're going?" Danni asked Luke hopefully.

"I don't know, princess. But we'll soon find out. Let's go."

Luke and Danni piled into their jeep and sped down the same road behind the police cars that had disappeared in front of them.

Chapter Twenty-Three

Bill glanced at his gas gauge and saw that he had about an hour's worth of fuel left. He had passed over the Mexican border off the coast about five minutes before, and now listened intently as he scanned the frequencies for his next directions. He didn't have to wait long -- he soon heard a man's voice over the crackling airwaves telling him which direction to proceed and the exact coordinates of his intended landing site. The voice described it as a long, flat area on top of -- *a mountain.*

"Oh great," he said to himself as he imagined trying to land in such terrain. Were these people truly crazy? Did they really want their money or did they want to take a chance on it burning up inside the plane when it crashed with him in it? Then he decided it didn't matter anyway, there was no turning back now. He would do whatever was necessary to get Jessica back, or die trying. Whatever the Good Lord had in mind for him at this point was fine.

Stop! Go back!" Danni screamed in Luke's ear as he slammed on the brakes, trying to keep the jeep's rear wheels from swerving off the edge of the cliff.

"I think we should have turned off the road back there...where those tire tracks are," she said as she pointed off to the side of the road behind them.

Luke backed up as instructed, and then took in the rough, rutted trail that led up to the base of a nearby mountainside hovering over the ocean. "There? Are you sure? I'm worried we might get stuck, even in this jeep."

"It's too late to worry about things like that, Luke. Now drive. Hurry!" Danni instructed him firmly.

Luke shrugged and turned the wheel sharply, guiding the jeep over the bumps and lumps in the direction Danni pointed, thankful they had chosen this type of all-terrain vehicle.

Within twenty minutes, Luke and Danni had reached the base of the mountain, and they now knew for sure that they were not alone. Parked right next to them was a battered old army truck, but it's passengers were nowhere to be seen. They got out of their jeep, and Luke walked over to feel the hood of the truck.

"It's still warm. They must have gotten here not long ago."

Danni nodded in agreement, and scanned the mountainside in front of them for signs of life. Without a word, she began climbing up the steadily sloping embankment, headed for the top. Luke shook his head, unsure of where this would lead them, but he knew in his heart that he would follow his wife wherever she went at this point. It was her mind that was guiding them, and had gotten them this far.

They grabbed at protruding shrubs and bushes, pulling themselves up the rocky incline hand over hand. Twice Danni stumbled and Luke had to help her regain her balance before they continued on. It was early afternoon now and the heat was beating down upon them unmercifully. But despite the sticky sweat running down their necks and backs, Luke and Danni kept on climbing with only one thought in mind: Jessica.

When they finally neared the upper edge of the mountain, Luke held Danni's head down low as they took in the sight before them. There were two men huddled together about 100 feet away from where Luke and Danni hid. As they talked and gestured with their arms, they parted slightly and Danni gasped out loud as she saw the young girl sitting on the ground between them, hugging her knees to her chest. "Jessica."

Luke clamped his hand over Danni's mouth before she could say more, and prayed that the men had not heard her exclamation. Danni turned her head and nodded her understanding and apology for her outburst, indicating she would keep her voice low. They spoke together in whispers, keeping their heads below the edge of the large rock formation they were hiding behind.

"Oh Luke, it's her! She's alive!" The smile on Danni's face nearly broke Luke's heart in two as he thought to himself how unlikely it was that Jessica would live through what was about to happen, not to mention the two of them.

"Yes, bella. Thanks to you we have found her. But now we must think carefully before we decide what our next move will be. Both of the men are carrying guns and I'm sure they wouldn't hesitate to use them -- on Jessica or on us."

Danni nodded, and turned to peek out around the rock to watch the men once again. They seemed to be looking skyward as if searching for something -- a plane. They were there to meet a plane. That was why they had chosen this particular mountaintop -- it was very flat and long and narrow -- just like a homemade landing strip.

Danni whispered her conclusions to Luke, who agreed with her assessment. Then she added, "Isn't there some way we could let the Captain know where we are? Or the air force or somebody?"

"Unfortunately, I'm afraid not." Luke answered thoughtfully. "We'll just have to do the best we can by ourselves. Now the obvious thing we need to do is draw their attention away from Jessica. Then, since it looks like she's not tied up in any way, she'll run away from them and we can take her to safety."

"Okay, and how do we get their attention?" Danni asked hopefully.

"I don't know. I haven't figured that out yet."

"Great going, Detective Reghetti. Remind me not to count on you next time I'm in the middle of foiling a kidnapping." Danni stammered, her adrenalin making her heart race wildly.

"Let's hope there'll never *be* a next time, love," he responded.

Danni was about to speak again when they suddenly heard a faraway sound...a humming or droning noise. Luke squinted into the horizon and then pointed out over the ocean. "Look. Over there." he whispered. "A light plane is heading this way. That must be the one they're waiting for."

They watched together as within minutes the plane grew closer and closer, and finally banked to come in for a landing. They couldn't see who was in the plane, or if it was more than one person as they secretly hoped. But they were both mesmerized as they watched the brave pilot try to maneuver his aircraft towards a safe landing on this precarious plateau.

Danni found herself holding her breath until she saw the small plane bounce to a stop with only about fifty feet to spare before tumbling over the edge of the mountain where they lay hidden. The props slowly stopped spinning, and the pilot's door opened, a familiar figure stepping out.

"It's Bill!" Danni said softly in Luke's ear.

"Yes, and it looks like he's got the money for them in that briefcase he's carrying." He thought for a moment more as he watched Bill walk over towards the two men and his daughter, then told Danni, "Wait here while I circle around to the side. In exactly two minutes, start throwing small rocks towards the far side of the plane. While they try to figure out what's happening, I'll try to surprise them from behind."

Without waiting for her to acknowledge his instructions, Luke set out in a crouched run, his gun ready.

Then everything happened so fast and seemed so confused that Danni would always have difficulty describing the events that transpired. The two men were talking in earnest with Bill now, who was edging closer and closer to his daughter. Jessica seemed oblivious of what was happening around her, and Danni guessed that she was in shock.

Suddenly, Danni realized her two minutes was up, and she began hurling stones one after the other towards the side of the plane as Luke had told her to do. At the same moment, Bill began struggling with one of the men (the nicer of the two, Danni remembered later), and Luke came sprinting out into the open pointing his gun at the kidnappers and screaming for them to hold their fire.

Either the other man (the mean, ugly one) didn't understand English very well or didn't care to, because he fired two quick shots towards Luke which instead managed to hit the plane. Danni heard herself scream as she stood up in plain view. Luke then ducked behind the fuselage of the plane and fired one shot at the kidnapper, who dodged it easily. The smell of leaking fuel spilling out of the holes in the plane permeated the air, but no one took notice.

Before Luke could react, the worst thing happened: the more aggressive of the two kidnappers grabbed Jessica and held her to his chest with one arm while waving his gun with his other hand. "Viene aqui!" he ordered Luke, who slowly got out from beneath the plane and walked towards them. The man barked orders to his friend and the other man came towards Danni, indicating she should join them in their happy little group.

Bill's breathing was coming in ragged breaths now, his chest heaving. "If you hurt her, I swear I'll kill you with my bare hands." he threatened the man holding his daughter.

The man's hideous laughter rang out over the hillside, finally getting lost amidst the sounds of the pounding waves of the ocean down below. Then, ignoring the words of the girl's father before him, the man told his accomplice something in guttural Spanish that made him turn and disappear over the edge of the cliff.

Luke edged closer to Danni and whispered in her ear. "He's going to get a boat ready. They must be planning to escape by sea." He nodded towards the airplane next to them. "They couldn't leave by air now anyway, that's for sure."

"Callate!" the man holding Jessica yelled at them violently to be quiet. He gestured for them all to back up towards the edge of the cliff. Danni glanced back over her shoulder at the rocks below where the waves crashed, sending white froth bubbling into the air.

They must have the boat hidden in an inlet at the base of the mountainside. The coast along here was probably full of protected areas to slip a small boat into, she guessed. She thought sadly that it would be ironic for her to die in this way, at the hands of the ocean that she loved so much.

Luke was desperately trying to think of a way to rush the man without taking the chance of Jessica getting hurt at the same time. Not to mention Danni and Bill. It was just too big of a chance, he decided sadly.

The smaller man returned moments later and nodded towards the one holding Jessica, indicating the boat was ready for them to depart. A wicked smile spread over the man's pockmarked face, showing his crooked yellow teeth to their worst advantage. He slowly pointed his gun at Luke and said, "You will be the first to die, señor, since you try to be the bravest. You should have gone home when I tol' you to."

"The note at the inn in Rosario," Danni gasped, and the man nodded, his beady eyes mere slits in his scarred face. Danni vividly remembered the terribly evil feelings she perceived when she first saw the note, and knew she was looking at the source of that evil.

Just as the gun was leveled at Luke's heart, another shot rang out from somewhere behind them. The kidnapper's gun flew out of his hand, and he momentarily released Jessica to massage his wrist where the bullet had seared him.

Bill leaped forward and grabbed his daughter, shielding her from further danger with his life. The smaller kidnapper was just raising his gun to take charge when a voice called out, "Jose'! No!"

Everyone turned at once to see the originator of the shout and the shot. Walking towards them, a rifle in his hands, was Martin, followed by Maria, a look of fear mixed with anger on her face. Luke took the opportunity to rush over and pick up the kidnapper's gun that had landed several feet away, and then retrieve his own gun also. He rejoined the group just as Martin began to speak to the smaller of the two kidnappers, who was handing over his own gun without a fight.

"Jose', I cannot believe you have done this terrible thing."

Danni leaned close to Luke and said softly, "Now I know why he looked so familiar to me. That must be Martin's brother."

Maria nodded in their direction and then spit on the ground in front of her brother-in-law. No words were needed from her to convey her feelings towards the men who had done this to her little one. Maria then ignored everyone else and rushed to throw her arms around Bill and Jessica, tears running down her brown cheeks as she murmured words of solace to them both.

Luke was guarding the other kidnapper, who they soon found out was named Luis Fernandez just as Danni had predicted. Martin was screaming at his brother in rapid Spanish, too rapid for Luke to understand. But it wasn't necessary to know exactly what was being said. It was obvious to everyone that Jose' was getting an earful from his brother. Danni just stood and watched the whole scene unfold before her, feeling the exhaustion from endless days of worry and strenuous concentration overcome her.

A few minutes later, the sound of three large police helicopters filled the air above them and they saw that help was on the way. Luke smiled as he realized that the Captain had figured it all out somehow and now they would all be safe. Jessica could go back home, and he and Danni could go on their delayed honeymoon. What a relief!

Chapter Twenty-Four

Peggy sat across from Luke and Danni at their kitchen table, sipping from her glass of Sterling Merlot as she listened to their story, amazed by their experience. "Wow! You guys could make a T.V. movie out of this. It's unbelievable."

Danni smiled at her crazy friend who had gotten her into this whole thing, but then reminded herself that if it hadn't been for her involvement, she would never have met her wonderful husband, Luke.

"Well, I don't know about that, but I'm just glad that everything worked out okay and that Jessica is safe now," Danni said.

Luis and Jose' had been transported first to the Mexican jail, and then extradited to the United States where they were being held on charges of kidnapping. The authorities were trying to see if they could press for the death penalty under the Lindbergh Law, which was passed in 1932 as a result of the kidnapping and death of famed aviator Charles Lindbergh's infant son. But the law only applies if a person is abducted and transported across state lines -- and a death occurs. So, they might have to settle for a long imprisonment sentence.

179

The story had come out as to why Martin's brother had participated in the crime to begin with. It seems that Jose' had lost his job several months before and was desperate for money. When he had run into Luis and it was discovered that Jose's brother worked for a rich Americano, the plot was hatched to kidnap the young girl and hold her for ransom.

The reason it had taken so long for them to issue their kidnapping demands was because of Jose's immediate concern over what they had done. He had wanted to return the girl to her family as soon as he realized how serious the whole thing was, but Luis had told him that he would tell the police it was all Jose's idea and place all the blame on him. They had argued back and forth for the first few weeks, until finally Luis won out and the first ransom note was delivered.

It was then that Martin had become suspicious, and had soon found out that his brother was involved in something bad. He still hadn't realized his brother was responsible for the kidnapping -- that idea was just too outrageous for Martin to believe. He had thought Jose' was into smuggling drugs or something like that, but not a crime against an innocent young girl.

When Martin had finally found out what he had dreaded was true, he had struggled with his conscience as to what to do next. He desperately wanted Jessica back, but at the same time he didn't want his brother to go to jail. He knew he couldn't tell Maria or she would go right to the police. It had been a terrible time for him.

Finally, he had decided to go down to find his brother in person and try to bring Jessica back himself. It was the only thing he could do, but he didn't know that his wife would follow him there. When she caught up to him in Rosario, he had to listen to her yelling and screaming for an hour before he calmed her down and told her his plan to confront his brother. Maria had demanded to go along, and he was unable to convince her otherwise.

The police had questioned Martin and Maria endlessly, then finally decided to release them, as they believed their story of noninvolvement in the crime.

Brad, on the other hand, was safely ensconced in a cell himself, awaiting a preliminary hearing to set bail on his charge of issuing a fake ransom demand. He had at least hoped to hear from Nancy after his arrest -- it was all her fault that he was in this mess in the first place, he told himself. After all, he only did it to get the money to make her run away with him so they could be happy together. But to his dismay, there was no sign of Nancy or anyone else for that matter. Since he couldn't afford an attorney, he had to rely on the court-appointed representative for his defense.

Jim had returned two days after everyone else, smiling from ear to ear as he introduced his new wife, Shirley. It seemed that he had fathered a child by Shirley some thirteen years before and had always wanted to make things right between them, but never had the courage to do so before. Then, seeing the suffering and pain surrounding all those who loved little Jessica, it made Jim realize how fleeting life really is and he decided to find Shirley and his daughter before any more time was wasted. Shirley had been thrilled to take him back and get married. She had never met another man that she loved as much as she had Jim, and their daughter was a lovely young woman just approaching maturity.

"The pictures on his wall." Peggy chimed in gleefully.

"Yep," Danni said. "Here I was so sure he was some sort of a child molester and all the time they were pictures of his own daughter. That shows what a lousy psychic I am."

Luke took her hand and kissed her palm lovingly. "You may be a lousy psychic, but I'm crazy about you, princess."

As Danni and Luke kissed, Peggy grimaced and complained, "Oh, good grief. Here we go again. Aren't you guys ever going to settle down and behave like normal married people? All this lovey-dovey stuff is sickening."

Luke and Danni laughed at their friend, then Peggy added, "And you can't be serious about being a lousy psychic, Danni. After single-handedly finding where Jessica was being held and making a spectacular rescue."

Luke frowned good-naturedly, and said, "Well, I don't know if she did it 'single-handedly'. I did have a little something to do with it, if I recall."

Peggy waved aside his comment and added, "I think you should make this your new profession: 'Psychic for Hire: Criminal Investigations My Specialty'."

Luke smiled and reminded everyone, "Hey, I'm the one who first thought up the perfect name for Danni, if you recall: 'Psychic Princess'!"

Danni groaned at their patter, and they all toasted to their beautiful future. A future that Danni just knew held much happiness and excitement for them all.

Epilogue

Dr. Smith now straightened and solemnly picked up his notepad, tucking his pen neatly back into his inside coat pocket. As he slipped into his overcoat, Danni began to worry he was overwhelmed with her story, and wouldn't – or couldn't – possibly believe it was true. He surprised her when he looked at her and smiled, gently.

"I don't think there is anything wrong with you, my dear." He straightened his tie and went on. "Frankly, if more people were as in touch with their inner selves as you are, this world would be a much better place."

"But, Doctor, don't you think it's strange that..." Danni began with concern in her voice.

"No," he interrupted her as he placed his free hand reassuringly on her shoulder. "There is nothing strange about the God-given talent you have been given. Just use it wisely, and follow your heart."

He walked to the door to let himself out. "And for Heaven's sake, don't ever listen to anyone who tells you that you're a fake, or doesn't believe in you. Stay strong and true to your beliefs, and you will be fine."

As she watched him close the door behind him, Danni found herself saying softly "Thank you…" but he was already gone.

Suddenly both dogs were yipping at her feet, and the cat was whining for food, as usual. Danni shook her head and smiled, reaching down to pet them. "Guess I'd better go finish that sculpture now, before I get into any more trouble!" she told her pets lovingly.

Jörgen Andersson

Leanna Burns

About the Author

Jolinda has published several other works, including her "Soul Survivor" novel and her poetry compilation entitled "Inspirations." She is currently working on some new books in the metaphysical realm. (Watch for "Angel Words" coming soon.)

Jolinda lives with her husband in California near her hometown of Santa Barbara.

Jolinda's main goal – *in this life* – is to heighten others' awareness via the written word as to choices and circumstances we all face as we travel the path towards our destiny. You are invited to join her in this quest by reading her novels and poetry.

Visit Us Online at **www.SummerlandPublishing.com**